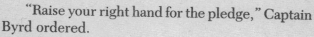

"Raise your right hand for the pledge," Captain Byrd ordered.

David raised his hand.

"Repeat after me, but give your own name . . . I . . ."

"I—David Monroe," David said, hearing the cacophony of more than thirty other names around him, "do solemnly swear that I will support and defend the Constitution of the United States against all enemies, foreign and domestic; that I will bear true faith and allegiance to the same; and that I will obey the orders of the President of the United States and the orders of the officers appointed over me, according to the regulations and the Uniform Code of Military Justice.

"So help me God."

David lowered his hand, awed by the solemnity of the oath.

"At ease," Captain Byrd said. "Dismissed, and good luck, soldiers."

"We'll need it," someone behind David whispered as he filed out of the room behind Carver.

Standing Tall, Looking Good

Gloria D. Miklowitz

Published by
Dell Publishing
a division of
Bantam Doubleday Dell Publishing Group, Inc.
666 Fifth Avenue
New York, New York 10103

ISBN: 0-440-21263-4

RL: 6.3

Reprinted by arrangement with Delacorte Press

Printed in the United States of America

July 1992

10 9 8 7 6 5 4 3 2

RAD

Acknowledgments

WRITING A BOOK about three young people who go into the U.S. Army was the idea of George Nicholson, vice-president and publisher of Delacorte's Books for Young Readers. I loved the idea at once, but worried how I could capture on paper the day-to-day life of a soldier going through basic training without having experienced it myself. What do recruits talk about in the hour before lights out? What's it like to fire an M-16? To undergo a poison gas attack? What does a drill sergeant talk like when he's trying to turn eighteen-year-old kids without discipline into dependable soldiers?

To find out, I first visited the Pasadena army recruiting office, where Sergeant Gerd N. Hoffmann told me how young men and women are recruited. Through the veterans' affairs office of Pasadena City College I made contact with recent veterans Eric Anderson, David Christopher Andrus, and Rick Major, who individually visited my home and for hours shared their army experiences, both good and bad, with me. Two women—Marian Smith, Spec. 4, serving at the Presidio in San Francisco, and Stacy L. Morgan, Spec. 4, at Fort Ord, California—gave me

Acknowledgments

the female perspective. Sergeant Donald Barron at Fort Ord was also interviewed.

Kathleen Ross of the Public Affairs Office of the Army in Los Angeles, and Paul Stone of the Los Angeles Recruiting Office were extremely helpful in setting up interviews, answering questions, providing written material, and in reading this book for technical accuracy. Finally, my appreciation to Marcel Hicks from Pasadena High School, who gave me the portrait for Carver Williams.

My thanks, my appreciation, to all these kind and generous people.

Standing Tall, Looking Good

CHAPTER

1

☆

"DA-VEY! COME OUT OF THERE! The company's here!"

David folded a T-shirt and laid it on the bed beside the overnight bag. "In a minute, Mom!"

"Must you be contrary up to the very last! This party is for you, remember?"

"In a *minute*!" he repeated, straining to sound patient. His last night home and they were laying this stupid party on him. What he would have liked was a quiet family dinner, laughing together, remembering good things, maybe with Bree included. But it didn't work that way, not when you didn't like each other much, so maybe this was better. Anyway, a few more hours and he wouldn't have to put up with it anymore.

He heard his mother's exasperated sigh, heels clicking down the hallway, and then whispered words to Charlie, his stepfather, whose deep, angry response gave him a moment's satisfaction.

David stuffed an extra pair of socks into the overnight bag along with underwear, a sweater, and his shaving kit. For a long moment he stared at the framed photo on his bedstand of himself and Bree taken at the prom two months ago. They made a good-looking couple—Bree in a blue strapless dress with the pearls he'd given her and him in that rented monkey suit with the wide white cummerbund around the middle. His hair looked good, too, thick and shoulder-length the way he liked it; he was glad he'd held out against his mother's nagging to have it cut.

He pressed a forefinger to his lips and touched Bree's face on the picture. It would be a while before he'd be back to sample the real thing again. And then he slid the picture under the box of stamps and stationery his little sister, Heather, had given him and the Tom Clancy novel he hoped to read on the plane and closed the lid.

That was it.

Just a few hours more of being polite and keeping his mouth shut around his mother and Charlie and then . . . And then it's *bye-bye American pie*—or however that song went—*you're in the army now.* He jumped to his feet and saluted himself in the mirror, but his stomach felt like he'd swallowed a lead ball and his tongue like leather. Fixing a smile on his lips, he opened the bedroom door and went downstairs to the party.

"DAVID, *darling!*" his aunt Cyn cried as soon as he showed his face in the living room. Eyes turned his way, smiled, but conversation went on. These were mostly relatives he hardly knew and Charlie and his mother's friends, not his. "Come here, darling! Give this old lady a great big hug!" His aunt opened her short, chubby arms inviting him into a bosomy embrace. Grinning, he strode across the room, lifted her hundred and seventy pound bulk, then set her down as she blustered protests, laughing and red in the face.

"Al, sweetheart!" She turned to a tall, thin man at her side. "This is that handsome nephew I told you about. Would you believe I used to diaper this big, strapping fella when he was just so big?" She held her hands apart to show how small David had once been. "You know," she added, with an impish grin, "once, when I was changing him—"

"Auntie!"

She laughed, pleased at David's discomfort. "Oh, Davey. How can you do this to us? How can you disappoint your mother and Charlie so? They had such great plans for your future. Joining the *army*! It's crazy! It's insane! Only poor kids, kids without choices, do that!"

"I thought your generation was against war," Al offered.

"You could be going to college! You could be planning for a nice career. You could go into law, join Charlie's firm . . ." his aunt went on, warming to the subject. "What possessed you?"

"Oh, I don't know," he quipped, playing it light, though her words hit a nerve. "I just passed the army recruiting office one day and thought—*yeah!* Why not?"

When he'd told his mother and Charlie that,

(3)

they'd blown a fuse. Charlie had rolled his eyes to the heavens. "Just the kind of impulsive, stupid thing you always do!" his mother had cried. "Anything to spite me!"

There hadn't been a breakfast, lunch, or dinner since without arguments. Charlie even tried playing understanding stepfather, inviting him to play tennis one Sunday (prompted by his mother, of course), but by then his obstinacy had hardened to rock, as it always did when they wanted what was "best" for him, which always turned out to be what would look "good" to their social set.

"I *know* what's best for me, Auntie. Honestly," he said, with almost no irritation in the tone. His eyes wandered above her head looking for an out. "Besides, it's done. Be glad for me, okay? Mom and Charlie will be better off with me gone." He chucked his aunt under her chin, bent and kissed her forehead. "Nice meeting you, Al. See you later, gorgeous. There's Bree."

"HOW YOU HOLDING UP?" Bree whispered, brushing his lips with a quick kiss. He slipped an arm around her waist and would have maneuvered her out of the room except that he remembered the promise to his mother.

"Have you noticed?" he asked Bree. "Except for us, no one here's under forty. And it's supposed to be *my* party."

"You *did* celebrate with the crowd last night . . ."

"So I did." He smiled, remembering what he and Bree had done afterward. "Gonna miss me?" He took her arm and steered her to the table full of platters of meats and cheeses, caviar and shrimp on ice, handed her a plate and took one for himself.

"Miss you? I'll probably forget you. Three months before you get leave! Two years away! That's a looong time!" Bree smiled sideways at him.

"You better not forget me!" He lifted a shrimp with his fingers and stuffed it in his mouth. "I won't see food like this for a while!" He glanced up to see Charlie watching. *Use toothpicks!* his stepfather mouthed. He turned his back. Man. They never let up. If you put all their rules in a book, it would be thicker than the Bible.

Bree led the way to the piano. "Are you scared? I'd be petrified."

"Me? Come *on!* The Daredevil?" He chuckled. In their circle of friends he was the the first to try anything risky, the only one who'd gone hang gliding.

"Liar . . ."

He didn't answer. There were so many things he *was* afraid of, he didn't want to think. Like what it would be like away from home for the first time. Like how he'd get along with the other guys. Like whether he'd be able to hack being told what to do every minute of the day when he was used to doing things his own way in his own time. Ever since he'd signed up he'd had misgivings. But darned if he'd admit he might be wrong. And see Charlie smirk?

"The only thing I'm afraid of is whether you'll still like me," he said. "You know—the Rambo image, and all?"

"Ah, you're a pussycat, underneath. You won't change. Besides. You'll look gorgeous in a uniform."

Smiling, he took a seat beside Bree on the piano bench and dug into the mound of potato salad on his plate. "I might look good in a uniform, but will you still like me—almost bald?"

"NOW THAT WASN'T SO BAD, was it, David?" The last guest had left; the caterers were cleaning up. His mother kicked off her heels and dropped down on the white living room sofa. She lifted Heather's sleeping head onto her lap and stroked her daughter's thick dark hair.

The cozy scene almost choked him up. It reminded David of a time long ago in a smaller house before his father ran off.

And then Charles came into the room. "It's late," David answered. "The recruiter will be here around three-thirty. I better get some sleep."

"Stay a minute," his mother said, an unaccustomed break in her voice. "There's so much we haven't talked about . . ."

He glanced at Charlie loosening his tie, watching. Even that small gesture irritated him.

"Honey—put Heather to bed, will you?" his mother said to Charlie. "David? Come sit here." She patted the seat beside her.

"It's awfully late, Mom." He glanced at her, and felt a flood of love for the freckled face that looked so vulnerable and young. "What do you want to talk about?" he asked, sitting down.

She took his hand and pressed it to her lips. "I just want you to know that we love you. I know you don't quite believe it. You think Charles and I are your enemies, but we're not. We only want the best for you. And now you're going. I can't quite believe it." Tears welled in her eyes.

"It won't be forever. I'll have leave in a few months, after basic."

"Charles says, if you find it too tough you don't have to go through with it."

Charles says. *Charles* says. His mother idolized the creep. Didn't she know that whatever Charlie said, he'd want to do the opposite? "I'll be okay."

"But if you *should*. . . . We'll help you all we can."

"I'll be *okay*."

"Of course you will," his mother hurried to say. "You're a *man* now." She stroked his hand and swallowed him up with her eyes. He wished she meant what she'd said, but the way things had been this last year he'd done everything to thwart her and Charlie —and it made him look like a rebellious hood, not a man.

"I better go, Mom," he said, getting to his feet. She clung to his hand. "I gotta get up in three hours."

"Wake me when you do. I'll make us some fresh coffee before you leave. Just the two of us!" She picked up her shoes and stood beside him in bare feet, gazing lovingly at him. Poor Mom, he thought. Caught in the middle.

"No, Ma. It's okay. I'll have coffee at the MEPS station. Don't get up." He put his arms around her, surprised that her head came only to his chin, and hugged her tight. "I love you, Mom. This is what I want. Please don't worry; I'll be just fine."

"Of course he will," Charlie said, coming back into the room and breaking the mood.

He pulled away from his mother as if he'd been caught doing something wrong. "Thanks for the great party. I gotta get some sleep." He pretended a yawn. " 'Night, you two. And *don't worry*." He patted his mother's arm, turned and strode out of the room without looking back.

He slipped into Heather's room and turned on the bed lamp to look down at his ten-year-old sister. "Hey, rabbit," he whispered, calling her by his pet name. "I promise to write. Really." He bent low and kissed her forehead.

In his own room he undressed quickly, set the alarm, and then lay in the dark staring at the ceiling. Charlie wasn't all wrong. What a dumb thing he was doing—signing his life away for two years just to get away from home.

2

IT HADN'T BEEN QUITE AS SIMPLE as he'd told everyone—that he'd just walked into the recruiter's office on a whim.

What really happened started at school one day. Over the loudspeaker came the announcement that there'd be a special assembly third period. If you wanted to hear an army recruiter, you'd be excused from class.

Far out! he'd thought. He had algebra third period and hadn't finished the homework.

He went to the auditorium and slumped down in the seat, arms crossed over his chest, half listening to the conversations around him. Johnson, the principal, followed by a guy in uniform arrived and climbed the steps to the stage. David yawned, and closed his eyes.

"Let's have it quiet!" Johnson boomed. He rapped the mike with a pen so that it made a raucous sound followed by a squelch of feedback. David opened his eyes just long enough to see that the soldier Johnson introduced as Sergeant Walker had dark hair and a mustache.

"Anyone who doesn't want to be here, go on to your regular class," Johnson announced. Then he turned the mike over to Sergeant Walker.

"Good morning, ladies and gentlemen," Walker began.

"There are no ladies here," a joker nearby whispered, getting a few laughs.

"I'm here to tell you about the career opportunities for both men and women in the United States Army."

For a while David let the words wash over him, the fact that there were around 360 different jobs you could be trained for, that you could serve in many parts of the world, that you got paid well while in the service and had free room and board, medical and dental care. Even the part about patriotism had a certain appeal. It was when Walker got to the educational benefits that he opened his eyes and sat up.

"Sign a two-year contract and you can walk away with more than $17,000 in educational benefits. Sign on for four years and you've got $25,200!"

The hum of uninterest among the students had quieted to absolute silence. David leaned forward, eager to catch Walker's every word. *Money for education!* He wouldn't have to be indebted to Charlie! He could earn his own college money, study what *he* wanted, and show that creep his mother had married that he could make it on his own.

The auditorium lights were turned out and the audiovisual department showed two short films—one about army life and the other about a vocational aptitude test that each enlistee would have to take. When the lights came back on Walker said, "In the past we promised a lot more than we delivered. Now, we guarantee—*in writing*—that whatever you want to study, wherever you want to serve—you get it. No problem."

"Wow . . ." David whispered to himself.

"Any questions?"

A kid near him raised a hand. "Where's the catch? You give away all that money for just *two years*?"

"Right. And afterward you're in reserve for six more in case your country needs you."

War. It could mean serving during wartime, David thought with a quick rush of adrenaline.

"You, over there!" Walker quickly went on.

"What about women?"

"I think they're *wonderful*!"

David felt an easing of the tension around him in the laughter that followed. He figured Walker probably used that line regularly for just that purpose. "About ten percent of our army is female," he continued. "It's a great place to learn important skills, to grow up and earn money at the same time, and to gain that terrific educational bonus for when you get out . . ."

"Don't be snowed by all that rubbish," a kid nearby whispered. "Would you like killing peasants in Central America?"

"What about the *communists*?"

"Sssh!" David hissed, wanting to hear the answer to the next question. "Is the army like—*Rambo*?"

Walker chuckled. "No way!"

"What about basic training? I hear it's real tough."

"It *is* tough," Walker said. "I kid you not. Some can't take it and some can't make it. But if a couple of million guys—and girls—got through it so can you."

By the time David walked out of the auditorium with a handful of brochures, his head was spinning. Most of his friends were going on to college. He hadn't even applied, not just because Mom and Charlie wanted him to, but because he was sick of being shut away in classrooms after twelve straight years. And he didn't know what he wanted to study anyway.

Maybe *the army* was the answer!

That very afternoon he'd gone to the recruiting center and taken the first step.

HE HADN'T TOLD A SOUL, not even Bree, what he was up to, not until he was sure. He was going to play it smart. Show Charlie and his mother that he could think things through for himself. If the army was going to get him for two years, he was going to be sure he got whatever was his due. He wasn't going to sign a thing until he knew precisely what he wanted. And not until he got a written guarantee he could have it.

"You'll graduate from high school in June?" the recruiter had asked.

"Right."

"Ever been arrested for possession of drugs? Been in jail?"

"Nope."

"Then if you're sure, we'll set a date for the physical and vocational aptitude tests. They'll help us decide what you might train for. It's a pretty full day of tests so we'll put you up overnight. Two weeks from today, okay?"

It was when the sergeant went over the results of his test that he'd nearly pulled out.

"Nice to meet you, David," Sergeant Montoya said that day at the Military Entrance Processing Station called MEPS. He extended a hand across the desk and gave him a friendly smile. "Now let's see what your scores say." He bent to study the folder in front of him. David sat tall and stiff, trying to read the pages upside down. He'd studied the career manual cover to cover before taking the test. He didn't care what the scores said; he knew precisely what he wanted to sign up for.

"You did very well," Sergeant Montoya said, smiling. "You rate especially high in the mechanical skills area. The army needs men like you to operate tanks, fly helicopters, build bridges, launch missiles . . ." He referred to a computer printout. "How about training for engine mechanic, or aircraft maintenance. These are some of the jobs you might do well at." He turned the sheet around for David to see. "Any of these look good to you?"

David scanned the list briefly and shook his head. "Not interested." He'd spent enough time studying the career book to know that a lot of the job titles looked pretty, while the jobs themselves were often nothing much. Like the guy who ladled food out from behind a counter was called a "food specialist."

Montoya bent over the papers again. "You did pretty well in verbal comprehension. How about something in business and clerical? Ever think about going into law? Become a paralegal?"

And be like Charlie? "No thanks!"

"Do you have something specific in mind, then? Just what *would* you like to be?"

"M.P.—military police!" he blurted out, and then sat back, glad it was out. It was not only as far away from what Charlie did as he could think, but that's what his real father did—only as a civilian policeman in New York.

"Yes, well—there are no M.P. slots open right now. You'll have to choose something else or wait for a slot to come open."

David felt as if he'd been punched in the stomach. He'd done a lot of soul-searching before he'd figured out what he wanted. "I see," he said, with a mixture of disappointment and relief.

"How about . . ." Montoya said, and he rattled off other options, trying to make them sound alluring.

David stood up. "I don't think so. No thanks. It took me a long time to make up my mind and you don't have what I want." He felt good that he handled himself so well.

"Just a minute," Montoya said. "I'm sure we can find something you'd like . . ."

"No . . . no. If I decide I want anything else, I'll be in touch."

By this time he seemed to have gathered an audience. Two other sergeants joined in the battle for his body. They really wanted him; it made him feel important and in control. "We put you up overnight, you know . . ." one said, in an intimidating tone.

"I don't owe you a thing!" he cried.

"Of course you don't," a woman sergeant said. "Look, David. Give us just a few more minutes of your time. I'd like you to see a film. It's about the Rangers. They're like the Green Berets, the army's special forces. Rangers are part of our infantry. Maybe this will be what you're looking for."

He shrugged. What was another few minutes?

He let himself be led into a viewing room and sat through a film that kept him riveted to his seat. Yeah! The Rangers! That's what he wanted. It would be even more exciting than being an M.P.!

The woman sergeant took over, and in the next half hour he signed his name to the army contract for two years enlistment in the infantry, with specialized training in the Rangers. He left the MEPS station with a date to ship out and a scared, excited feeling in the pit of his stomach.

And then he'd gone home and told everyone.

CHAPTER

3

PAULA

AS SOON AS THE BELL RANG, Paula Carlson
plucked up her books and strode out of the classroom. She had precisely a half hour to get to her job,
which meant a mad dash to the state college parking
lot, a harried drive over the pass into Westwood, and
finally, the hassle to find parking.

On the freeway the traffic moved steadily. She
settled back, turned on the radio, and relaxed. At this
rate she'd make it to the Good Earth for her job,
waitressing, in time. But as she pressed her foot on
the accelerator for the uphill climb, she felt a fright-
ening hesitation as the car lost power, surged, then
hesitated again. "Not now!" she mumbled aloud.
"Oh, please don't quit on me now!"

She'd put over three hundred dollars into the old
car in the last two months, money she couldn't afford,

not when she had to pay toward the rent and food at home, not to mention the fees at school, car insurance, and all the rest. What if it was the *transmission*? That could be terribly expensive! Where would she find that kind of money?

Coming up behind her was a red Honda, closing in, demanding in car body-language that, regardless of her problems, she pick up speed or pull over. "Well, I can't!" she cried. "You'll just have to wait or move around!" She pressed the gas pedal to the floor, leaning hard against the safety belt as if her own body could force the car forward. Again the car bucked, and then, miracle of miracles, surged ahead.

Unwanted, the tears started then, running down her cheeks so that she had to reach with a free hand into her purse for tissues. She'd thought college would be fun. She'd imagined sitting in the cafeteria talking with others about Life, going to football games and dances. Instead, it had become a nightmare of keeping up with assignments late at night or in the few spare weekend hours. Fellow students had suggested she *buy* her research papers, as *they* sometimes did when crowded, but she couldn't see what she'd learn if someone else did the work.

It wasn't only school, though. Breaking off with Dan, two months ago, had been the hardest thing she had done in her life. She couldn't even think about it now without feeling a wrenching pull in her chest.

She turned off the freeway onto Wilshire and concentrated on melding left so that she could turn up Glendon to the public parking lot near the hospital. At the traffic signal she let her eyes drift to the people, mostly UCLA students, crossing the street. The odds of seeing Dan were, of course, infinitesimal. She knew that. Yet each time she arrived in Westwood her senses became more alert and her pulse nearly doubled as she scrutinized every tall, blond-headed man on the crosswalk. And then, with a sense of loss and disappointment, she would drive on.

LATER, when she came out of the kitchen with a tray of chicken salad sandwiches and cheese enchiladas, her eyes took in the new people who had taken tables in her service area. She sucked in her breath and nearly stumbled. Dan! He was seated at one of her tables, menu in hand, watching. So! Why was he here? What did he want?

Stop it. Control yourself, she told herself. *It's over. Move!*

She delivered the sandwiches and enchiladas, so rocked by her feelings that she couldn't make the small conversation that always brought bigger tips. Legs trembling, she moved to Dan's table, order pad ready.

"Hi," he said in the familiar deep voice that she loved.

"Hi," she said in reply, trying to sound business-like. His dark eyes smiled, reaching deep into her, but she stiffened.

"How you been? I've missed you. We need to talk."

"There's nothing to talk about." She felt her face grow warm, and concentrated on the pad. "Would you like to order?"

"Paula, please. Give me a chance to explain! I've been miserable without you."

Not half as miserable as I've been without you, she thought. But no. She wouldn't put herself through that again. Dan was bright and good-looking, interesting and fun, but irresponsible and self-centered, undependable and charmingly unfaithful. Over the months she'd excused most of his faults, but the one thing she wouldn't put up with was his roving eye. "Dan, please. Let's not go through this again. Especially not here." She realized as soon as the words came out that she'd given him an opening.

"Where, then? I'll meet you anywhere you say." His intense, sincere eyes almost made her doubt.

"We've been through this already. No."

"She meant nothing to me! Honestly!"

Neither did the others, she thought. "No." The pain in her throat was unbearable. "Do you want to order?" She looked directly at him, willing her face to hide any signs of distress.

He stared at her for a long moment, a puzzled look on his face, and then picked up his books. "No." He touched her shoulder as he passed. "See you around."

That evening as she left the restaurant to go home, she heard two students talking, behind her. "The rewards are fantastic," one of them said. "Sign up for four years and you've got over twenty-five thou for college afterward. And you can write your own ticket on what you want to learn."

"But it's the army," the other said. "Who wants to go in the military?"

"I don't know. If there's no war, would it be so bad?"

She'd had to cross the street, so she didn't hear the response. Suddenly she no longer felt tired. Was that the answer? Go into the army? Was that the way to an education without all this hassle? Did they offer careers in journalism? She could hardly wait for to-morrow. There was a recruiting office right near the college. Tomorrow, she'd have some answers.

CARVER

"YOU GOT SOME MONEY, Son? I'm cold broke till payday and Kisha needs new sneakers."

Carver Williams hesitated. This was when she usually got him, just as he was headed out the door to school. He reached into his back jeans pocket for the worn wallet. "Ten enough?" The look on his mother's face said it wasn't, so he took out the rest of his money until payday—a five and five singles—and handed it to her.

"Thanks, sugar. I'd ask Deon . . ." his mother said with a small, apologetic smile that made her look almost girlish. "But I know you don't like that."

"Yeah." Good-bye twenty bucks.

Deon was his mother's latest boyfriend, a smooth-talking, good-looking dude who dealt drugs. He dressed well, drove a white Mercedes, and knew how to spend the money he made from being a pusher.

Carver knew about dealing. A lot of the guys in the neighborhood and at school made their living that way, which was all right if that's what they wanted. As for him, he'd seen so much misery—friends dying, and even little kids, his own people hurting their own—that he'd have nothing to do with the stuff himself.

Carver understood his mother's need, too, and that Deon could have any woman but had chosen her —a thirty-two-year-old. Being Deon's woman gave his mother a kind of status in the building, and to

Deon's credit, he made no effort to push drugs on her.

What bothered him about Deon was none of those things, but that sometimes his buyers came to the apartment. And while Carver saw plenty of spaced-out kids on the streets and at school, he didn't want any of those crazies in his space, especially not near Kisha. And he didn't like Kisha being bought off, like his mother, by all Deon's dirty bucks. Or getting the kind of looks the dude turned on his fourteen-year-old sister lately.

These thoughts filled his head as he walked to school. It was the last semester of his senior year, and a deep discontent had crept into his soul these recent weeks so that nothing he did gave him joy anymore. Not even Lavonne, that sweet-natured girl he loved.

When he tried to sort it out, he grew angry.

"What is it eatin' away at you, honey?" Lavonne had asked the last time they were together.

"Nothin's eatin' away at me," he'd said, in a voice full of anger at her noticing.

They'd been sitting in the living room at her place, watching a video, and she'd raised her head from his shoulder to peer into his eyes. "What you so angry at me for, Carver Williams? You *know* I'm right!"

He usually hid his feelings under a mask of cockiness. When a teacher asked where his homework was one day, he slumped in his seat and said, "I offed it in the microwave." The class roared and the teacher shook his head and turned to someone else.

When did they think he could do homework? He worked thirty-five hours a week bagging groceries and spent another twenty-five or thirty in school.

The only time he could do the reading and writing they were always piling on him was the period before it was due, which wasn't always possible. He had no intention of explaining that to a teacher.

With Lavonne, though, he didn't have to act smart. She knew him as well or better than he knew himself.

"I been thinking about when I get out of school," he said finally, turning down the TV sound.

She tucked her long, pretty legs under her slender body and studied his face. "You not thinkin' of quittin' again?"

"Maybe." He shrugged. "Might just as well drop out. I'm not learning anything. What difference would it make?"

"Aw, honey," Lavonne said. "Don't talk like that."

He was glad she didn't lecture him, like the counselors did, about getting that diploma and the doors it opened. That was so much crap! All a high school education got you was a job for minimum wage, if you were lucky. Even the guy selling tires at Fedco had a college education.

"I'm no great student. You know that," he said, taking Lavonne's hand.

"Grades aren't everything. You're smart, Carv! You are! You could get all A's if you wanted. Teachers been telling you that for years and askin' how come you don't 'live up to your potential.' "

He shrugged. She always found a way to make him feel better, but this time it hadn't worked.

"You could go to community college . . ."

"Sure, and *still* have to work for spending money. How would that be different from what I'm doing now? Aw, shoot!" He shrugged off Lavonne's comforting touch. "I'm sick of everything. I'm sick of sleeping on the living room couch, of never having a little privacy. I'm sick of school and Mom, and Deon, and never having enough money . . ."

"You sick of me too?"

"Not you, honey. Never you." He leaned over and kissed her tenderly. Lavonne was the best thing that had ever happened to him. "Sometimes I think, though . . ." he added in a quiet voice, "maybe I'm just bashing my head against the wall. Maybe I should just do what Deon's doing. There's plenty of money and it's not hard."

Her eyes opened wide. "You wanna end up in jail? Or *dead*?"

"You know I was kidding. Don't look at me like that."

HE THOUGHT of that evening now as he walked to school. Was it true that he wouldn't? If he stuck around this neighborhood long enough, maybe he would. Half the guys around either dealt drugs or had someone in the family who did. What made *him* special?

What he really wanted wasn't so very much, really. Why was it so hard to get? All he wanted was to make a decent living at something he liked doing so he could take care of Kisha and his mom, and— Lavonne.

Was that so much to want?

CHAPTER

4

IT WAS STILL DARK when David heard Sergeant Walker pull up and park outside. He jumped to his feet, grabbed his bag, and hurried to the door before the sergeant could knock and wake the family.

He'd slept badly and awakened before the alarm rang, so anxious he couldn't even stay in bed. He showered and dressed and rechecked the contents of his overnight bag a dozen times before going down to the kitchen to fix himself instant coffee and peanut butter sandwiches. The minutes had dragged by and finally he'd gone to sit on the bench no one ever used in the entry hall, waiting in the dark, adrenaline surging each time the clock bonged the quarter and half hour.

"I'm ready!" David whispered, opening the door to Sergeant Walker, waiting outside.

"Good. Let's go."

The streetlights were still on as he pulled the door closed and walked out to the car at the curb. The air smelled thick with smog, and he thought briefly that it would be hot and humid later. A dog barked in the neighbors' yard.

"Got keen ears," Walker said, unlocking the car trunk. "You got a dog?"

"Had one, but we put it to sleep a couple months ago." He threw his bag into the trunk, closed it quietly, and went to sit in front beside the sergeant. As the car moved away from the curb David looked back at the home he'd lived in since he was eight. No lights. They were all asleep. It brought a small lump to his throat but no regret. Then he turned to face forward. With a sense of exhilaration he realized that he was leaving everything that was dependable and familiar for everything unknown and scary. He sat back and took a deep breath.

IT WAS ALMOST FIVE-THIRTY and starting to get light when they got to the MEPS. The parking lot was as busy with private cars and vans arriving and discharging passengers as if it were midday. He lifted his bag from the trunk of Walker's car with hands that were cold and clammy.

"Well, soldier. This is it. They'll take it from here. You know where to sign in?" Walker asked.

"Yeah."

"Well, good luck, then. Be sure to stop by and say hello when you're home on leave."

A van pulled up as Walker drove off. The doors opened and girls and guys spilled out carrying their small bags through the double doors into the building. David followed.

"All those shipping out today check in at the Army Guidance Shop," he heard over the loudspeaker.

"Where's that?" someone behind him asked.

"I think it's this way." David turned to see a tall black guy wearing a T-shirt that said MUIR HIGH VARSITY. *Someone* from near home! he thought, pleased. "Follow me. You from Pasadena?"

"Yeah."

"I figured that. I'm from La Cañada!"

"Oh, *yeah*! Where the *rich* guys live."

He almost opened his mouth to make some kind of smartass comeback, but let it pass.

The holding room was full of young people sitting on vinyl-covered couches and chairs, talking, sipping coffee or colas. Announcements rolled through an electronic message board. Men and women in the uniforms of all the armed forces milled around and served behind the information counters.

"The lockers are this way," David said. "I remember from when I was here for the tests. We're supposed to stow our bags—*gear*, I guess we call it now— but keep our enlistment packets, I think. What color's your folder?" He led the way through the crowded room to the locker facilities.

"Red."

"Mine too. I think that means we get processed first. When's your flight out?"

"Twelve-thirty."

"Hey, same as mine! Where you going?"

"Atlanta—then to Fort McClellan."

"Me too! Infantry?"

"Yeah." The black guy smiled and stuck out a

hand, palm up. David slapped it. "Carver Williams . . ."

"David Monroe . . ." David dropped his bag on the floor beside others under the lockers. Carver did the same. Then they went on into the Army Guidance Shop.

"NAME?"

"David Monroe."

The soldier found his name and checked it off. "Let's see your enlistment packet." He riffled through the pages checking for verification of his high school diploma, birth certificate, social security card, and driver's license. "Any changes since you filled this out?"

"No."

"Any recent speeding tickets? Any run-ins with the law? Any bills you left unpaid?"

"No."

The man signed his name on one of the sheets and sent him across the floor to the medical desk. He found two seats side by side, hoping Williams would be coming soon, and glanced around. There were about a dozen others waiting for their medical check, mostly guys and a couple of girls, He looked the girls over with casual interest. Not bad-looking, but nothing like Bree. He wondered if there'd be any women at McClellan. Probably not. Williams slid into the seat beside him. "Hurry up and wait, right?"

"We're not doing so bad. Six-thirty and we're already here. The day I signed up I didn't get my physical until after one."

"How long you in for?"

"Two years. You?"

"Three."

"I'm going into Rangers," David said, feeling a satisfying pride. "What about you?"

"Aircraft mechanics. I figure as long as they're willing to pay me while I learn, I may as well train for something I can use when I get out. With all the old planes around these days, I shouldn't have any trouble getting a job."

"Yeah." David nibbled a thumbnail, aware Williams had struck a nerve. Charlie had said, "If you're determined to go into the service, at least sign up for a career you can use later."

"I like *excitement*," he'd said, emphasizing the last word deliberately because he thought Charlie's work was so dull. "Like my *dad* . . ." he'd added, knowing it would hurt. "I can become a policeman, go into security, maybe . . ."

"If that's what you want," Charlie had said, his voice dropping to resignation.

"Monroe, David!" the nurse called.

"Here!" David jumped to his feet and waved his red folder. They'd called him before others because of the flight.

"Follow me."

He went through the same procedure as before. Height. Weight. Blood pressure. Vision. And then he saw a doctor who checked his nose and throat, shone a light in his eyes, and listened to his heart and lungs. He asked David the same questions about drug use and general health he'd been asked the day he'd signed up. And then the doctor initialed the health form and sent him back to the guidance shop.

"Man, the paperwork!" David exclaimed when Carver Williams joined him. "They must have a pound of forms on me alone. Between lawyers, like my stepfather, and the government, the planet's going to fall out of orbit from the sheer weight of paper!"

Williams laughed. "Relax. We may as well get used to it."

"Those of you leaving on the twelve-thirty flight for Atlanta form a single line and step forward," one of the sergeants announced.

David joined the six guys who stood up.

"Brown. Lee. Monroe," the sergeant read from his list. "O'Neill. Telemantes. Williams." He looked up. "Anyone with previous military experience?"

No one raised a hand.

"All right! Then I'm going to pick one of you for group leader." He glanced around. He read David's name tag. "You. Monroe! You're in charge. These are the airline tickets. Count them. Six. It's up to you to see that these guys—every one of them—get on the bus to the airport, and on the right flight to Atlanta. Understand?"

"Yes, sir!"

"Good. Now move on out to the waiting room until the next swear-in!"

David accepted the packet of tickets and took his position at the front of the line. It felt funny, being in charge. Why had the sergeant picked him? Did he look older, wiser, more like a military type? It felt funny, but in a good way.

Maybe it was because he was in charge that he paid more attention to the other five in the group. Williams had settled back on the couch in the holding area, cola in hand, eyes closed. Lee and Telemantes had already formed a friendship, having driven in from Ventura on the same bus. O'Neill chewed gum and looked over the magazines on the table. Brown went off to the men's room. "They're going to call us in a minute," David warned. "Make it fast."

"Listen up! Next swear-in in five minutes. Room B129. Form a single line and file in," the voice on the loudspeaker announced soon after.

"Hey, Brown's still in the john," David announced to the others, checking down the hall.

"No sweat. He'll hear it in there," Carver said.

"I better get him. You guys go on. Save us seats." David strode across the room to the men's room, opened the door and called, "Brown? You here? They called for swear-in!"

Brown came out of a stall. His eyes were red and swollen. "I'm not going. I changed my mind."

"Hey . . . I know how you feel. I felt that way this morning too. Come on. We'll be late." He took his arm, but Brown shook him off.

"I'm not going! It was a mistake. My father talked me into it. I've never been on a plane! What if it crashes? Those guys are all jocks! I'm not like them!"

"Ah, come on." David placed a hand on Brown's back and steered him outside. "We're all a little scared. There's nothing to flying. It's safer than driving the freeway. And don't worry about measuring up. Sometimes the toughest-looking guys turn out to be marshmallows in the crunch."

He'd gotten him out of the bathroom and talked him down the hall. Brown still resisted, but did what he was told. They were the last ones to check in before the sergeant shut the door.

"Okay, listen up!" a soldier said, walking to the

desk in front of the room. "Only those whose names I call should be here." He called off the names of thirty-five people, some standing around the back of the room.

David kept his eyes on Brown, seated in front of him. Maybe he shouldn't have talked him out of leaving. Who did he think he was—God? On the other hand, wasn't that what he was supposed to do as group leader?

The sergeant droned on about the procedure for traveling to the different bases, and the airlines each group would take. He rushed through a list of articles about the penalties for fraudulent enlistment, desertion, and AWOL. David's mind wandered and his eyes drifted to a slender redhead in a seat two rows away. What a beauty! Skin like cream and hair the color of fire. She wore a green T-shirt and jeans. He wondered where she was from and where she'd be going and why someone like her would join the army. When she turned his way, his face grew warm.

They filed into the adjoining room, row by row, and formed lines in front of a podium. The redhead stood right in front of him, almost blocking the flags —six—one for each of the services, the army, navy, marines and air force, plus the United States and California.

He listened intently as the sergeant explained the swear-in procedure and how to stand at attention and at ease. And then a captain walked in and took over.

"Raise your right hand for the pledge," Captain Byrd ordered.

David raised his hand.

"Repeat after me, but give your own name . . . I . . ."

"I—David Monroe," David said, hearing the cacophony of more than thirty other names around him, "do solemnly swear that I will support and defend the Constitution of the United States against all enemies, foreign and domestic; that I will bear true faith and allegiance to the same; and that I will obey the orders of the President of the United States and the orders of the officers appointed over me, according to regulations and the Uniform Code of Military Justice.

"So help me God."

David lowered his hand, awed by the solemnity of the oath.

"At ease," Captain Byrd said. "Dismissed, and good luck, soldiers."

"We'll need it," someone behind David whispered as he filed out of the room behind Carver.

CHAPTER

5

HE SAW THE REDHEAD AGAIN, lined up to board the airport bus, and passed her on his way to a seat in the back. She had green eyes, and some freckles that made her look wholesome and young. When she caught him looking, she turned her face to the window.

The six of them found seats together, with Brown beside O'Neill and Williams taking the seat beside him. Brown seemed to have calmed down, but David figured he'd better keep an eye on him, just in case. Regular mother hen, he said to himself, suppressing a grin.

His pulse picked up as the bus entered the airport circle and stopped at each of the terminals. With each stop, fewer people remained. He gripped the handle of his overnight bag, ready to leap up as soon as they reached United. Finally, the bus pulled up to the terminal. He led the way down the aisle and stepped out to the curb. In front of him, disappearing through the automatic doors, he glimpsed the red-head.

"We've got over an hour before flight time. Let's find out what gate we're leaving from," he said when the group reassembled. "Then get something to eat." He was glad he'd learned *something* from Charlie, if only how to find his way around an airport.

He threw his bag on the X-ray scanner and stepped through the security check. Most of the others hesitated, as if they'd never gone through the procedure before. They followed until he'd checked them in at the gate and led them to a nearby snack bar.

"Where you from, Brown?" Carver Williams asked when they'd settled at a table with their sandwiches and drinks. He popped the top of a cola can and poured it into an ice-filled paper cup.

"Inyokern."

"Where's that?"

"Near China Lake—you know, in the Mojave?"

"I been through there," O'Neill said, lighting up a cigarette. "Nothin' but sand, cactus, and jackrabbits."

"Hey, O'Neill. Kill the butt, okay? No smoking, see?" David pointed to the sign nearby. When he saw Carver's disgusted smirk, he felt like saying, Listen, guy! I'm supposed to keep these guys out of trouble, right?

"There's lots more than sand and cactus out there!" Brown's pale gray eyes focused on O'Neill. "My dad *works* at China Lake for the Navy Department; he's an aircraft mechanic."

"What's the navy doing in the *desert?*" Carver asked.

Brown's protest could barely be heard over the laughter. "The navy's not just ships! They've got an air force too! They design rockets and stuff there!" He looked from one to another of them, begging understanding.

"So, why didn't you join the *navy?*"

Brown's lips twisted into a small, embarrassed smile. "I get seasick."

"So why don't you work in the desert like your old man?"

"I'd like to, but most enlistees serve on ships."

David listened to the debate over the comparative benefits of the different services, but his mind lost its concentration when he saw the redhead enter the snack bar with two other women. She bought coffee and a sweet roll and checked around for a place to sit. He half stood and pointed at the empty table next to them, but she didn't seem to notice and took a table near the exit.

"May as well forget that one, Monroe. They're not gonna let us near any chicks for at least two months!" Carver smiled a slow, insinuating grin.

"I've *got* a girl!"

"Don't mean a thing. Does it, guys?"

"*I* got a girl," Telemantes said. "Prettiest little thing you ever saw." He pulled out his wallet. "Look."

"How about you, Williams? You got someone?" David asked, anxious to turn the attention away from himself.

Carver considered only an instant whether to share Lavonne with anyone and decided not. That

Gloria D. Miklowitz

Monroe was the kind who had it easy from the day he was born. Papa a lawyer. Living in La Cañada. All the right connections. Probably go into officers' training and never know you anymore. And here he was trying to be "one of the guys." Why would someone like him join up when he had the world in his pocket?

He tilted his chair against the wall and swigged a long drink before answering. Then, fixing David with a cool, enigmatic smile, he said, "Me? Got a woman? Hell no. I got . . ." He made a kissing sound and held up three fingers.

THE REDHEAD and her friends arrived soon after at the waiting area for their flight.

"Looks like that cute redhead you've got the hots for's headin' for Atlanta too," Carver announced from the seat across from David. He shrugged his head in Paula's direction. It gave him a kick to see the way the rich white boy blushed at his words.

David swung around and saw the girl checking in at the desk for the same flight as theirs. An electric pulse ran down his arms and legs. He turned back to face Carver, pretending he didn't care.

"She's looking our way," Carver reported.

"Good for her."

"Probably has a thing for good-looking black dudes," O'Neill said, winking at David.

"Probably has," Carver admitted lazily. "But I like mine dark, real dark."

David chuckled with the others, but he was beginning to really dislike Carver. The guy had a chip on his shoulder. He was cocky, too smooth. When they were all having lunch and David had talked about hang gliding—how beautiful it was up there,

(36)

how you felt like a bird—the other guys hung on his every word while Carver looked bored.

"Ever go hang gliding?" he'd asked, trying to be friendly.

"Nope."

"When we get leave I could take you. I got a friend with a glider. We sail off of Mount Wilson." He realized even as the words came out that he must sound too eager, even boastful.

"No thanks, man," Carver had answered with a yawn. "I get enough excitement just trying to stay alive."

David had forced a smile while the others laughed. He wished he'd never opened his mouth.

And now the black guy was doing it again.

The loudspeaker announcement came at just the right moment. Their flight would be boarding. David jumped to his feet, picked up his bag, and rechecked the clutch of tickets. "This is it. Let's go, guys."

HE DIDN'T GET TO TALK with the redhead until after dinner was served. He'd stayed in his seat baby-sitting Brown until he was sure he'd be okay. The kid seemed so young. A hairless face and a runner's build. His skin had turned gray when the plane taxied down the runway, and he gripped the armrests during takeoff as if they were life preservers. His lips had turned blue at the thud made by the landing gear retracting. But now that they were flying at thirty thousand feet and dinner had been served and the sky outside was already turning dark, Brown had fallen asleep.

David climbed over Carver's long legs into the aisle, stood a moment to get his balance, and then ambled unsteadily toward the back of the plane and the toilets.

Lee, two seats back, had headphones on and tapped fingers to the music he heard; Telemantes thumbed through a magazine. O'Neill sat farther back in the smoking section. When David reached his seat, he saw three empty liquor bottles neatly lined up on his tray.

"Hey, Monroe!" O'Neill's voice rang out over the drone of the airplane.

"Excuse me . . ." The man beside him climbed over O'Neill into the aisle, giving him a nasty look.

"S'awright. Hey, Monroe! Pull up a chair and have a drink."

"Go easy, O'Neill," David said, lowering his voice. "Remember what they said in L.A. We're not supposed to get in trouble."

"Hey, listen, man! I don't need no mama telling me what to do. Why d'ya think I left L.A.?"

"Sssh!"

"Sssh y'self!"

He lingered in the aisle, not sure what to do. Should he tell the stewardess not to serve O'Neill any more drinks? Did he have the right? What the heck. It wasn't his business anyway. All he'd been asked to do was see these guys all got to Atlanta. In a couple of hours there'd be someone else to give orders. He left O'Neill and went on down the aisle.

She was standing near the window in back of the plane, watching the sun set, when he came out of the john.

"Hi." He felt that same scared excitement at seeing her that he'd felt the first time. "I saw you at the MEPS. I'm David Monroe."

Paula turned slowly, knowing before even seeing that the deep, pleasant voice would be his. "I'm Paula Carlson," she said, annoyed at the quiver in her voice.

"Where do you think we are?" He moved beside her to look out the window.

"I don't know. Texas? It's pretty flat down there."

"Maybe." For a while he gazed down at the golden plains marked by straight ribbons of roads. "Feels strange, doesn't it?" he said. "Like we're not quite a part of the real world. Sometimes, when I'm on the ground and see a plane like this flying by, I wonder who's inside. Where are they headed? Why? And I think their fates are bound together like ours, whether they ever speak a word to each other."

She flashed him an appreciative smile. "I've had that feeling too."

They stood in companionable silence gazing out of the small window. It felt good. Right. "What's a nice girl like you doing in the army?" he asked.

"What's a nice guy like *you* doing in the army?" she shot back, immediately defensive. Just the kind of sexist remark she'd expect from Dan!

He tipped his hand in a salute. "Where's your sense of humor, woman? I was just teasing." He smiled disarmingly. Man, she was prickly. Was it him, or what? Bree would have laughed at his little jibe. "You going to Benning or McClellan?"

"McClellan."

"Me too!" He stepped imperceptibly closer, feeling as if they were the last two people in the world. "Maybe we'll see each other . . ."

"I doubt it!"

A minute ago she'd been friendly. What was she

trying to say: *Bug off, I don't like you?* He considered returning to his seat. It was becoming dark outside and the cabin lights had been turned off. "Well," he began, checking down the aisle. "Looks like they're starting the movie."

"I'm sorry. I didn't mean to be so rude," she said. "It's just that basic's really tough, I hear, and I have plans. I want to be a journalist and I've got to pass basic to get the special training and educational bonus. I won't have time for anything else." She paused, suddenly aware she was talking too fast. His intense gaze unsettled her. "And you?"

"Just wanted to get away from home, be my own man for a change."

"Oh!" she said in surprise. "But why? You didn't have to leave home for that. I've been on my own since I was sixteen." That was when her dad had died, and her mother's salary hadn't stretched for two.

A flight attendant squeezed by, carrying the last of the dinner trays. "The movie is starting shortly . . ."

David nodded but made no effort to move. "I admire your independence, Paula. I've had it easy, too easy. My stepfather's an attorney. We live pretty well, but it's on his money, which means he calls the shots. I need to find out if I can swing it on my own."

"What will your specialized training be in?" She put a finger to her cheek and studied him. "Let me guess. Food prep?"

David rolled back on his heels and laughed. "I can't boil water! Hell, no! I'm signed on for Rangers." She'd probably think he was big on brawn, small on brains; the Rambo type, hardly the kind she'd go for.

"Like Green Berets?" Her face grew serious but her eyes brightened with interest. "That's dangerous!"

"Not if you know your stuff." He stood straighter and smiled. "Movie's starting."

"Yes," she said distractedly. "Better get to our seats." She brushed by him, almost running down the aisle. There was something about the kind of men who sought out adventure and danger that had always appealed to her, maybe because physically, she considered herself a coward.

"See you again . . ." he said. She can't stand me, he thought.

She slid into her seat, reached for the earphones and pretended to be interested in the movie, but her heart would not settle down for some minutes. Now stop that, she admonished silently. *You put that man out of your head this minute!*

David returned to his row and climbed over Carver's feet again to get to his seat. He busied himself showing Brown how to find the movie channel on the armrest controls. That Paula was something. Imagine, being on her own since she was sixteen!

Carver yawned and stretched his arms above his head. "Score?"

"Aw. Bug off," David said.

CHAPTER

6

IT WAS LATE IN THE EVENING and dark by the time they arrived in Atlanta. "Jeez!" David exclaimed as soon as they left the air-conditioned terminal and felt the heavy, hot air outside. "It's like a swamp!" He pulled off his windbreaker and stuffed it into his bag. Perspiration soaked his shirt, and his trousers clung to his legs.

"Keep together!" he called behind him, moving along with the crowd of young people, recruits from all over the country, gathering around the buses at the curb.

"Buses to Benning to the left; McClellan to the right! Move it! Let's go!" a man in uniform called.

He climbed onto the first available bus, making sure first that there were enough seats for all six of them, and dropped down in a seat near a window. "Brown! Over here!" He pointed to the place beside him, as much to keep an eye on the kid as to avoid having to sit beside Williams again.

"What a madhouse!" Brown stowed his bag in the overhead rack. "How long a trip we got?"

"Three, four hours, I think. It's over the state line, in Alabama. Ever been to the deep South?"

"Never been out of California. Hey, it's raining!"

David glanced out of the window as the bus pulled away from the curb. He'd heard Atlanta was a beautiful city, but all he could see in the dark and with the rain pelting down were the headlights of vehicles moving toward them and the slant of rain caught in the glow of streetlamps. He felt lulled by the steaming heat of the bus, by the harmonica-playing recruit in a seat somewhere behind him, by the occasional laughter around him.

"You scared, Monroe?" Brown asked. "My uncle was in the service and he tells some real horror stories about basic."

"Yeah, a little," David admitted, able to say in darkness what he might not in daylight. "It's not knowing exactly what'll happen next."

"You see the size of some of these guys? I mean, a lot of them look like football players. Basic will be nothing for them!"

"You never can tell. . . ." David yawned, hoping Brown would take the hint and leave him alone. He needed time to think. He wasn't used to being surrounded by people every second of the day.

He rolled his jacket into a pillow, propped it against the window, and rested his head on it. Eyes closed, he tried to call up Bree's face, the way she tilted her head, the way her lips curled in a playful grin, but her image would not come. Instead it was the redhead's face he saw, the green, disinterested, almost insolent eyes. He wondered if she might be thinking of him in her seat, two rows behind, and smiled.

THE LAUGHTER, the cardplaying, the music, came to an abrupt halt several hours later as the bus left the pitch-dark of a woods and came into the lighted area of the Reception Center. David peered through the rain-streaked window trying to make out what the place looked like. It was in the middle of nowhere. He hadn't seen the lights of a nearby town in the last half hour. If he wanted to run—which was ridiculous, of course—where would he run to?

The bus slid to a stop, the lights went on, and the exit doors swung open. He felt the rustle of expectation all around him as he reached for his bag. A solidly built black serviceman hopped on the bus.

"Welcome to Fort McClellan. I am Sergeant Smith!" he announced. "Everybody—off the bus! On the double! Don't forget your personal belongings! Line up outside! *Now!*"

The aisle filled quickly with recruits pushing toward the exit. "Hey, it's pouring out! We'll get soaked!" someone behind David complained. "Poor baby," he heard, in a voice that sounded like Williams's.

"Move it!" Sergeant Smith shouted. "Get the lead out of your butts! You're in the army now!"

"Move it! Move it! Double time! Hup, two three four!" a duty sergeant shouted. "Line up single file! Let's go!"

David trotted along behind the guy in front, eyes forward. Rain ran down his face; water kicked up by the recruit in front splashed his pants. His shirt clung to his skin.

The sergeant led the recruits into a well-lit building and told them to file into the rows of seats, sit down, and keep their mouths shut. It was already after midnight. David longed for a hot shower and a clean bed.

"This is the McClellan reception station," a captain announced when everyone had settled. "You will remain here for three days during which time you will learn the first most important rule about being soldiers—*obedience*. Obedience without question! From now on you don't have your mommies and daddies to tell you what to do. From now on the only parent you have is the army. And the man who represents that army is your drill sergeant! It is your purpose in life to *please* him. You will obey him at all times. Without question, *instantly*. If he says 'jump,' you will jump! Never—I repeat *never*—do you question his order."

The captain paused, letting his words sink in, eyes sweeping the hundred or so trainees before him. "There is only one parent in this army—and he is your drill sergeant! Do you understand?" The captain cupped a hand to one ear.

"Yes!" David shouted with the others.

"Yes what?"

"Yes, *sir!*" the recruits roared together.

"Louder!"

"Yes, sir!"

"Good! Now, in three days you *grunts* have a lot to do. You'll be given more medical tests, and shots; you'll be issued uniforms and get haircuts! You will learn what you may not have learned at home—how to make your own beds and polish your own shoes! You will learn how to behave like *soldiers*! And, by golly, if I have to teach you myself—by the time you leave this Reception Center you *will* know how to march like a soldier! *Do* you understand?"

"Yes, *sir!*"

"Good!"

It was after one in the morning before the orientation ended and the new recruits were shown to their barracks. David wondered what Carver and the others thought about it all, but there was no time for conversation. There was no time for anything except following orders—making up the bunk, stowing his bag in the locker assigned, toileting—and then, abruptly, lights out and silence.

He lay on his bed, hands pillowing his head, staring up at the ceiling and listening to the breathing, coughing, snoring sounds of those nearby. They're going to wake us in a few hours, he told himself. *Sleep!* The oppressive heat, the strangeness of the day and place, and the lack of privacy kept him wide awake. Even the old tried and true methods of putting himself to sleep by thinking of Bree, failed.

It seemed like he had barely shut his eyes when the loud clattering began.

"Up and at 'em! Rise and shine, ladies!" The clash of garbage can lids continued. "C'mon, you grunts! Up you go! I want you washed and dressed and beds made in fifteen minutes, or you'll be pushing up the sky."

David opened one eye and saw a tall soldier marching between the rows of beds. He squinted at his watch. Three-thirty! Christ, it was the middle of the night! He pulled the sheet over his head and groaned.

"C'mon, Monroe. Get your white ass out of bed before you get in trouble!" Carver hissed. He yanked the sheet off David's body and tossed it at his feet.

"Leave me alone!"

"You got about twelve minutes, man," Carver said from the foot of the bed as he pulled on a shirt. "Less, 'cause here comes trouble right now!"

David bolted out of bed and grabbed his pants, but too late. The sergeant stood above him glaring down. "Are you deaf, boy?"

"No, sir!" David pulled his pants on without looking up, then stood at attention, barefoot and half dressed.

"You don't say *sir*! I am *not* an officer. I *work* for a living. It's Duty Sergeant Jones, boy. Understand?"

"Yes, sir! I mean—yes, Duty Sergeant Jones!"

"If you're not deaf, how come you didn't hear my orders?"

"I don't know, Sergeant Jones!"

"What's your name, boy?"

"David Monroe!"

"You a momma's boy, Monroe?"

"No, Sergeant Jones!"

"What did you say?"

David stood at attention, eyes on the sergeant. "No, Sergeant Jones!"

"Don't frig me, Monroe. You're a momma's boy all right. Or else . . ." The sergeant paused as if he'd just had a brilliant thought. "Or else—you're a friggin' queer! Which is it, Monroe?"

The heat rushed to David's head and he bit back

the words he wanted to say. "Neither, Sergeant Jones, sir!"

"If you're not a momma's boy, Monroe, and you're not a friggin' queer, then what are you, boy?"

"I don't know!" From the corner of his eye he saw Brown and Telemantes trying to make their beds, watching.

"He doesn't know!" the sergeant said, addressing the others with innocent concern. Then, with a vicious rush of words, he screamed, "On the floor, grunt! *Face*down." He pointed to the spot where he wanted David—between the rows of beds.

David dropped to the floor.

"Do fifteen!"

Fifteen what? he almost asked, and then realized he meant push-ups.

"One . . . two . . ." the sergeant counted slowly. "Three . . . Next time you hear *wake up* in this man's army you *wake up*, boy. Understand?"

David grunted, his body weight supported by his arms. *Count,* damn you, he begged silently, trapped in the uncomfortable position. Sweat dripped down his face.

"Four. Five! You—Williams!" he heard the sergeant say. "See that momma's boy Monroe does what I said!"

"Six. Seven. Eight. Come on, Monroe!" Williams whispered. "Don't quit!"

David had gotten to nine and dropped to his face, sweating, tears running from his eyes. "Can't."

"Come on, rich boy. Don't be such a marshmallow! My sister can do more push-ups than that!"

Arms trembling, David forced himself into push-up position once more. "Ten. Eleven . . ." At fifteen he rose unsteadily to his feet, dripping with sweat, sick to his stomach. He gave Williams a killing look and hurried to finish dressing. That Williams could go to hell. So could the sergeant. So could this whole friggin' army.

7

"NEXT!"

David climbed into the barber chair Lee had just vacated and stared glumly into the mirror. The barber wrapped a sheet around him and turned on the electric clippers. One more indignity. And to think of the argument he'd had with his mother about getting a trim for graduation!

It wasn't that he was particularly partial to long hair; the less wool on top, the cooler he'd be. It was just that the whole scene—a dozen guys in a row having their heads shaved—reminded him of a movie he'd once seen of sheep being shorn in the Australian outback.

He grimaced as the shaver made its first deep swath from back to front and back again. In the last hours he'd lost all sense of his own individuality. Eyes burning from fatigue, he'd moved with the others from place to place for medical and dental checks, uniforms and fingerprinting. He'd been poked at and jabbed with needles, sat through explanations on pay and allowances, survivor benefits, and the like and had filled out endless government forms.

"Next!" the barber called, flapping clean the protective sheet when he finished with David. David left the chair, running a hand over the smooth, shiny surface of his skull, and shivered.

"Cool, man . . ." Carver said as he moved to an empty barber chair.

"Yeah . . ." David replied, without enthusiasm. He eyed Carver's curly stubble. There must be a point to all this shearing. Hair was a way of individualizing oneself, like clothes. Without it, and dressed just like the next guy, the only way to stand out was to be a better or worse soldier. And after this morning's embarrassment, he was determined to be neither better nor worse—just invisible.

CARVER eased into the barber chair and grinned at the mirror. Poor rich boy Monroe; the expression on his face after he did the push-ups! The expression on his face now! Guys like him didn't know the first thing about humiliation. They didn't know what surviving was all about either. They were too soft, too used to being treated like little princes by everyone, even by their teachers whose jobs depended on being nice to the kids of rich parents. Not like where he came from.

He didn't know exactly what it was that pissed him off about Monroe, but he'd taken a dislike to him from the instant he found out where he lived. And then by his holier-than-thou attitude when he got appointed group leader and started giving O'Neill orders. Just let him try messing with *me*!

"Next!" the barber called.

Carver brushed the stiff bristly hair from his face and stood up. Except for skin color Monroe and he were equals now and in the army—skin color didn't count diddly-squat. Good. Now they'd see how well Monroe would survive the next eight weeks. As for himself—survival was his middle name.

DAVID dropped the last quarter into the phone coinbox and turned his back on the recruits waiting in line. He felt as nervous as if he were calling Bree for the first time. "Hello?"

"David? Is that you?"

"Sure is! You hear me okay?"

"There's a lot of noise on the line, but I hear. How's it going?"

"You wouldn't recognize me. I'm as bald as a bowling ball. All those gorgeous golden locks— gone." A lump grew in his chest and his voice cracked. Man, it was good talking with her.

"Miss me?"

"Are you kidding? Know what I'd like to do right now . . ." He curled into the phone, smiling.

Bree giggled and whispered, "Miss you too." Then she asked, "What's it like?"

"So far, bor-ing. We're at a reception center now. But tomorrow we go on to basic. I may not have a chance to call again, but I'll write. You write too, okay? It'll keep me from going crazy."

"Any women soldiers around?"

His face grew warm as he thought of the redhead. "A few."

"Pretty?"

"Uh-huh!"

"Behave yourself, soldier boy—or else. . . ."

The guy next in line poked his arm. "Time's up, Private."

He nodded. "Gotta go, Bree. *Write*, okay? Miss you!"

"Miss you too. Take care."

He left the phone wishing he'd asked Bree about home and their friends, wishing they'd been able to talk longer. Bree once joked she'd never make it as a nun. At the time, he'd laughed. Now he wondered. He'd signed up for two years. To Bree, that must seem a lifetime.

WHEN HE GOT BACK to the barracks it was almost time for lights-out. Most of the guys were polishing their boots, talking, going over the infantry manual, or writing home. He joined Williams and O'Neill, who were tossing cards faceup on one of the bunks while Brown watched. "What do you think it'll be like?" Brown asked, a tremor in his voice.

"You'll get through it," Williams said without looking up.

"Yeah, but what do you think it'll be like?"

"Tough."

"How tough?"

"How would he know, for Christ's sake, Brown?" O'Neill asked. "He's no more an authority than you are. It'll be tough. Okay? Maybe we'll have to run a hundred miles a day and do push-ups till we're blue in the face, okay? Stop being such a baby!"

Brown's mouth clamped shut and he picked up his infantry manual, averting his eyes.

"So, I was telling you," O'Neill went on, flipping another card onto the bed. "The counselor at the community college took one look at my grades and said—'Sonny, by the looks of these, you'd never make it. No use wastin' our time or yours.'" He laughed as if he'd made a good joke. "I hung around home a couple months till my pa got mad and threw me out, said, 'Get a job, or join the army.'"

"So you took the lesser of two evils, right?" David asked, settling on a bunk to watch.

"Right." O'Neill scooped up his winnings. "Bad luck, Williams," he said. "War's good for the economy, you know, creates lots of good jobs."

"Like building bombers and M-16s?"

"Yeah, like that."

"That's dumb, O'Neill. We could have a good economy putting people to work building things that don't kill—houses, cars, for instance," David said.

"You don't know what you're talking about, Monroe. We gotta be prepared. Those Commies are all around. Gotta stop them! Shoulda dropped the bomb on Vietnam. Woulda ended the war a lot sooner."

David whistled. "Man. Listen to the guy!"

"If that's how you think, why'd you join up?" Williams asked, throwing a card on the bed.

"I can love the U.S. without believing it's always right!"

"Better not tell that to your drill sergeant, Monroe." Williams picked up the cards and reshuffled them. "Or you won't make it through basic. No way." He chuckled, shaking his head.

* * *

THE FIRST CLANG of the garbage can lids was all David needed to become fully awake. He leaped from bed, trotted off to the head to wash and shave before the room became a mob scene with guys in line for the sinks, shaving with razors handed back from guys in front. He dressed, fixed his bed, and stood at attention with his two duffel bags ready—one full of military issue clothing and the other heavy with field gear. His shirt was already wet under the arms and on the back from the humid heat.

Outside, in the dark of early morning, he felt a nervous excitement, much like fear, as the empty trucks with long benches facing each other rumbled up the road to take them to the training camp.

"Atten-shun! You boys ready? Line up! First platoon behind Sergeant Smith! Second platoon behind Sergeant Collier! Let's *go!* Move it!"

David threw his bags on the truck and clambered on after them, heart pounding. Brown slid onto the seat beside him and Williams sat opposite, staring into space, arms crossed over his chest. As soon as every space was taken, someone slammed the tailgate shut and the truck took off in a roar of grinding gears.

No one spoke on the short ride to the training camp some minutes away. The truck made an abrupt turn, throwing David against Brown, and came to a stop in a parking lot already filling with recruits from other trucks. Someone yanked the tailgate down and instantly, like a pack of wild dogs, a dozen drill sergeants rushed at them.

"Get your f-in' asses out of there! On the double!"

"Move it, grunts! On the double! Get your friggin' bags and line up around that corner!"

"What you lookin at, lady? You think I'm foolin'? You think I won't kick ass? Get down on the ground and do ten!"

"What the hell you doin' down there doing push-ups, pretty boy! For Christ's sake, get off your face and get going!"

"A bunch of wussies we got here! Still on their momma's milk! Move it, wussy! Get the lead outta your feet!"

David grabbed a duffel bag in each arm, jumped off the truck, and without looking right or left in case he might catch the eye of any of the sergeants, trotted after Williams. He rounded the corner and came to an abrupt stop. Screaming and cursing all along the row of recruits were a dozen drill sergeants.

"Move, grunt! Move! Faster! My God, but you babies are slow! Stop there! Put your duffel bags down! Put your hands on your knees and face forward!"

"You! Fat boy! Man, we gonna trim you down to size! Get your butt up those stairs and I mean *fast*! *With* your pack, fat boy! Run! And keep it up till I say stop!"

"You! Down on your face and do twenty-five!"

"You!"

David had dropped his bags and sat unsteadily on the larger of the two, hands on knees, eyes on the distant flagpole. He didn't even glance sideways when he heard the sergeant screaming at someone two men away. His heart pounded and his head whirled and he thanked God that it wasn't him they were picking on. And then, suddenly, a tall sergeant whose breath smelled of onions and whose voice rasped like a buzz saw, stood in front of him. Maybe, if he didn't flinch, he'd go away. But the sergeant squinted his hate-filled eyes and brought his nose to within an inch of David's face. "You! Do you read me, soldier?" he screamed.

"Yes, Sergeant!"

"Do you know what you are, soldier?"

"No, Sergeant!"

"You are the lowest of the low! You are a mindless worm, a yellow-bellied grunt! You are so ugly I don't even want to see your face! Isn't that so, *lady*?"

"Yes, Sergeant!" Perspiration ran down David's chest. He wanted to punch the creep in the choppers, but all he could do was clench his fists and force them to stay in his lap.

"On your feet, meatheads!" the sergeant snapped. "Party's over! What do you think this is, summer camp? Get your asses up and move on down to the barracks! One two three four; one two . . . Step lively!"

David hoisted the heavy bags to his shoulders and hung on to them for dear life. He trotted along behind Williams, keeping the proper distance. Sweat ran down his face, tears of humiliation filled his chest. Why had he joined up? How stupid could he be? Was this what it would be like for the next eight weeks?

CHAPTER

8

CARVER LAY IN HIS BUNK after lights-out, hands under head. He heard the fire guard walking between the rows of cots, checking lockers, checking to see if anyone was smoking or writing letters in the semidark. He heard quiet breathing, an occasional snore, and the sound of muffled crying.

The day had been *shit*. A shock from the minute they hit camp. They'd been shouted at, cursed, forced to do endless push-ups, told they were stupid and worthless beyond belief. Even their manhood had been questioned. It had been a screaming, chaotic snakepit of a day where he ran when and where he was told, ate on command, pissed with permission, kept his mouth shut, hardly took a breath without wondering if he dared.

If he were to take it personally, he'd be in serious trouble. Others had. He could tell by their shocked faces. The only thing to do, he figured, was go along with the game because the army didn't care diddly-squat for wounded feelings. All that mattered was instant, unquestioning obedience. For eight weeks he could handle that. Anyone who couldn't—they'd break.

What he found hardest, he realized with a surge of pain, was the loneliness. There was no one here he trusted or liked enough to confide in, and Lavonne was three thousand miles away.

"PAULA?" the girl in the bed beside her whispered. "You awake?"

Paula considered not answering. She could hardly keep her eyes open. Between physical training and the emotional horrors of the day she needed to close it all out for at least a few hours. But she liked the blond girl from Georgia whom she'd met at the Reception Center. Christine, her name was, just barely eighteen, with a year-old kid and no husband. "Shhh. Yeah, I'm awake. What's up?"

"I hate it here!"

"Yeah. So do I . . ."

"I won't make it." Christine's voice broke.

"Sure you will. It's only the first day."

"I'm so sore! All over. I can't do all those sit-ups and push-ups! I can't! And I can't stand the way they scream at us all the time!"

"We all hurt, Chris. We're just not in shape yet. Give it time. Once we develop some muscles, we'll be okay."

"That Thompson must have trained at Auschwitz," the girl in the bunk below her whispered. "She looks like a man and acts like a Nazi."

(59)

Paula didn't answer. Drill Sergeant Thompson had taken special delight in going after her.

"Private Carlson. You didn't get a haircut!"

"It's not required, ma'am."

"You think you're so cute. If we cut that hair, we'll see how cute you'll be! Get a haircut!"

Paula had bitten her lip and stared straight into the sergeant's narrowed brown eyes. She had pinned her hair up, fulfilling the regulations of hair above the collar. She didn't care what Thompson said. She could not force her to get a cut. "I'm sorry, Sergeant."

"What did you say?"

"I don't want to cut it."

The sergeant's face had turned red. "She'll cut her hair or the rest of you will suffer," she sputtered. "This is the army, not a goddamn beauty school! Private Carlson."

Paula felt a flash of heat burn her face. The sergeant peered closely at her. "I don't like you. I don't like weak-kneed sisters who spend all their time primping in front of mirrors to be pretty for the guys."

I'm not like that, Paula wanted to say.

"Private Carlson. You know what I'm gonna do? I'm gonna turn you into a friggin' *soldier*! That's what I'm gonna do, and you betta believe it. I'm gonna *make a man of you*!" Her eyes glittered. "You betta believe it!"

Paula sucked in her breath to stop from saying, *Not if I can help it*, as the sergeant moved on.

TANIA, in the bunk below, had pegged Thompson perfectly, Paula thought.

"I miss my baby. . . ."

Paula closed her eyes at the heartbreak in Christine's voice.

"I miss his little snuffling sounds when he's asleep. I miss the sweet smell of him, the way he fits so perfectly in my arms. . . . I want to go home."

On the bus from the airport Christine had spoken proudly of why she joined the army—so she could support her son, since her own mother hadn't been able to support her children.

"Quit that, Christine!" Paula spat out sharply. "You're going to hang in there, like the rest of us, no matter how awful it gets. You hear? We'll help you. We'll help each other."

"I can't!"

"Yes—you—can!"

"Sssh!" Tania warned in a whisper. "Fire guard coming."

Paula clamped her mouth shut and closed her eyes. In a minute, she fell fast asleep.

DAVID woke to the clang of a pot being struck by a metal spoon. "On your feet, scumbags!" Drill Sergeant Baker announced, striding between the rows of bunks. "Haul your asses to the parade ground in fifteen minutes or you'll know what for!"

Four-thirty. Still dark outside. Bleary-eyed, David slid from bed, pulling on his sweats and tennis shoes almost in the same motion. He winced. Every muscle in his body screamed with pain. He'd thought he was in good shape, what with all the tennis he played at home. Apparently not. He felt like a cripple. Even bending to tie his laces sent a burning pain across his shoulders and down his arms.

Dressed and shaved, he gulped a canteen of water for the sweat he'd be losing and devoted the last five minutes to making his bed. The drill sergeant had shown them how to make hospital corners and just how many inches the cover was to be folded. But as hard as he tried, he couldn't get it right. With growing frustration and fear of being late, he tried again. For sure Baker would cuss him out. How the devil did Williams do it so fast and well? And what the hell difference did it make if the bed sheet was tight as a drum?

When he could do no better, he catapulted out of the barracks and ran to the exercise field to join his platoon. He fell in behind a tall recruit so he wouldn't be noticed.

"Monroe!" the sergeant's voice boomed out.

"Yes, Sergeant Baker!"

"Do you know what time it is?"

"No, Sergeant Baker!" David moved slightly so he could see the drill sergeant. A tall, stocky black man with a scar down his left cheek, he looked like he could swallow a tank and not burp. The sergeant held out a stopwatch. "It is four forty-six! You are one minute late!"

"I'm sorry, Sergeant!"

"Sorry doesn't cut it! When I say fifteen minutes, I mean fifteen minutes!"

David stared straight ahead, holding his breath.

Baker glared at him. "Drop for twenty-five! Now! And the rest of you too! Next time it'll be sixty!"

David and the rest of his platoon dropped to the ground and began counting push-ups while Baker stood above them, raging.

"You guys gonna learn *discipline,* or I'll know

why! In the next eight weeks you're gonna know your M-16s like you know your own names! You're gonna be so fit you'll do two-mile runs without even breathing hard! And by the seventh week, *if* you make it that far, you're gonna know so much about chemical warfare, tactics, rockets, and a whole lot more that you'll pass the Super Bowl tests—all twenty of them—with flying colors!" Now the sergeant's voice dropped to a threatening growl. " 'Cause if you *don't* pass—you can just figure on seeing my face for another eight weeks!"

"Damn you, Monroe," the guy to David's left hissed. "You better not be late again!"

For the next hour and a half the platoon did lunges and jumping jacks, sit-ups and push-ups, always under the sharp eye of Drill Sergeant Baker. "Ladies," he called them, "meatheads" and "maggots." He trucked down the rows pressing a boot on one soldier's back during push-ups, or standing over another to curse him out for not being able to do enough sit-ups. Sweat ran down David's head into his eyes and he gritted his teeth. "Thirty-nine. Forty. Forty-one," he counted doing sit-ups. O'Neill had given up. Brown lay flat, knees pulled to his chest to relieve the spasms as Sergeant Baker screamed obscenities.

"Forty-five, forty-six . . ." David counted, eyes tightly shut in agonized concentration. If Williams could do it, so could he.

And then they ran. Ran until he thought there was no breath left, felt his legs would surely fold—while Sergeant Baker called cadence. "One. Two—three, four, five!"

"One. Two—three, four, five . . ." he repeated with the others.

"Bravo Company don't take no jive!"

"Six. Seven. Eight, nine, ten! Sing it out and do it again!"

Ninety minutes later he limped back to barracks with the rest of the platoon for chores before breakfast. It was all so stupid, the fuss the army made about neatness. At home, he threw clothes into his drawers and usually left the bed unmade. Here, he had to fold every pair of shorts and socks, every shirt, just so, and space them according to regulation in his locker. Otherwise the drill sergeant might yank everything out and make him do it again.

After PT the first day, Sergeant Baker had appointed Williams squad leader. "He's got more guts than the rest of you," the sergeant had announced. "So I'm putting him in charge." Williams had scored highest in the number of sit-ups and push-ups, and had run faster than the rest of the squad, so he guessed he deserved the honor—if that's what it was. Nevertheless, it didn't seem fair. And Williams had it in for him—which meant life could be even worse than it was now.

CARVER felt a certain pride that he'd been chosen squad leader over ten guys, including the ones from L.A. Over Lee, who was probably the smartest, over O'Neill, whose attitude was rotten but who had a certain reckless spirit, or Monroe, who looked like Joe College. Still, the duties would isolate him even more. No one liked being told what to do, especially by someone his own age.

He wasn't sure if he could do it, either, if he could

be tough enough and still be one of the guys. If even one of them screwed up—it'd be his neck that was on the block.

"Listen up, guys," Carver said that first day as the squad stood at ease in front of their bunks. "I'm not gonna Simon Legree you. But you gotta do what you're told. I'll try to be fair. But whether or not you think I am, you do what I say. We gotta all pull together. I say empty the trash? No arguments, no questions—just do it. I say clean the latrine? Do it. 'Cause if you don't, the shit falls on me. And that don't make me happy.

"So, okay." He had looked around. "Brown, you sweep up; Telemantes, clean the showers; Lee put out the trash. Monroe—you wash the floor in the john. O'Neill . . ."

David didn't hear the rest. All he heard was that Williams had given him the worst job. *Tough guy from the Pasadena ghetto*, he thought, seething inside. Probably got kicked out of school for dealing. Probably was a pimp, what with three women on the string. *Gave me the dirtiest job!*

"Hey, Williams!" he called softly. "What's *your* assignment?"

Carver studied David for a long moment. Then he said, "I get to wash out the latrines. Wanna trade?" He smiled.

CHAPTER

9

WHY SHOULD I PUT up with all this crap? David mused, eyes closed during one of the dozens of army training films he'd seen in the last week. Who wrote those dumb movies anyway? They were worse than the stuff he used to see at school, when the teacher was too lazy to do a lesson plan. Films on how to apply foot powder, for Christ's sake! And who didn't already know about AIDS and VD? The only film that kept him wide-awake was the one on bayonet use, and even that was a bore. It showed bayonet techniques in slow motion, stop motion, every which way but inside out!

He slapped a mosquito on his arm and leaned forward in the chair to free the wet shirt stuck to his back. This place was the pits. Chiggers and mosquitoes big as bats. Heat and humidity so bad, you could hardly sleep at night. The lockers smelled of mildew.

At home, this time of year, he'd be surfing off Malibu, or messing around with friends. Last summer he'd had a ball, living with a bunch of guys in a rented house in Laguna, working at a stand selling corndogs, with enough time off for the girls and to swim each day. He must have been out of his mind leaving all that!

He opened his eyes. The screen showed the insignia for each rank of the army, while a narrator's voice described what was being shown. In case you're too dumb to read, he thought. Just like in the Smart Book, the little Army bible they were supposed to memorize. He closed his eyes and let his mind drift. Where was Paula at this minute? He smiled to himself at the thought that she might be right in the next room, watching the same film.

"Wake up, scumbag!"

David jerked to attention at the drill sergeant's voice. Sergeant Baker yanked him by the back of his shirt and glared down at him. "What's the matter, maggot? Didn't sleep last night? Don't find this interesting?"

"No, Drill Sergeant!" David took a deep, scared breath. The Monster was at him again. His heart hammered against his ribs and sweat poured down his face. He felt the eyes of the whole platoon on him.

"No, you didn't sleep last night? Or no, you don't find this interesting?"

"I was tired, Sergeant Baker."

"You're lying, maggot! You think learning about insignia is boring!"

"If you say so," David replied, too terrified to deny anything he might be accused of.

"Down on your face, scumbag! Do thirty! That'll wake you up!"

Thirty! He *couldn't*. Besides what he'd done in PT, he'd been down for push-ups every time he turned around these last few days. His muscles screamed at the abuse.

"One . . . two . . ." Baker called out as he dropped to the ground between the seats. "Keep counting, maggot! And the rest of you take note! Stay awake, or you'll be down on the ground with him!"

"Seventeen . . ." he counted, sweat pouring out of every pore. Through the wall of excruciating pain in his arms and shoulders he heard the voice of the film narrator. "As you can see, the rank of lieutenant colonel is designated by . . ."

"Eighteen . . ." He tried to block out the pain by thinking of what he'd like to do to Baker.

"Twenty . . . one . . ." His arms gave way. He could not lift himself one more time. He couldn't. The hell with Baker. Let him send him to the brig. Let him hang him, for all he cared. He couldn't do one more push-up. Panting, he rested his cheek against the wood floor. Tears rolled down his cheeks, along with sweat. He didn't even care what the others thought of him.

"Come on, Monroe!" someone whispered. "You can do it!"

He didn't have the strength to answer.

"Baker's coming back! Come on!"

"Only nine more, Monroe!" It was Carver's voice. "Come on! Don't let him get to you. You can do it. Up! That's it! Twenty-two . . ."

He didn't know if it was fear of Baker's return and the threat of having to do yet another ten push-ups, or Williams's anxious encouragement. He lifted himself one more time. "Twenty-two . . ."

"That's it! One more!"

"Twenty . . . three . . ."

"Only seven more! You're doing great!"

In the background the narrator's voice droned on: "The proper way to salute is to . . ." He was going to pass out. God, how he hated that drill sergeant. God, how he hated the army! "Twenty . . . eight . . ."

"Twenty-nine," Williams whispered, and then, with satisfaction, "thirty!"

"Permission to recover?" David managed to whisper.

"Permission granted!" Baker barked. "Williams?" David saw his face in the mirror-shine of the drill sergeant's boots as he struggled to his feet.

"Yes, Sergeant Baker!"

"Did I hear you whispering to this maggot here?" Hesitation, then, "Yes, Sergeant!"

"Drop for twenty, maggot! There'll be no talking when watching films!"

Now he'd gotten Williams in trouble! David wiped the back of his forearm across his wet face and stared wide-eyed at the screen, the narrator's words unheard. How could he stand it, but how could he quit? That's just what Charlie expected and his friends would say, "I told you so."

He stared unseeing at the screen and vowed, I'll be on time for PT if it kills me. I'll stay awake during class if I have to prop my eyes open with toothpicks!

CARVER COUNTED OUT the push-ups while asking himself why he'd come to Monroe's aid. Privileged rich kid! Couldn't even make a bed properly. Probably never had to. Got flustered every time the sergeant came near so he flubbed answers from the Smart Book more often than not. Out of shape, too. The first day he couldn't even do ten push-ups without passing out.

So, why did he care? What made him risk Baker's fury to help the guy?

The first answer that came to mind was self-preservation. If Monroe couldn't do the thirty, Baker would come down on *him*. He had anyway. That Baker was a prick, no doubt about it. Where *he* came from, a guy like that would have to be looking over his shoulder all the time if he wanted to survive.

Still—he had sort of begun to wonder if there was a reason for Baker's coldhearted meanness, for the constant barrage of punishment and insult. Could it be deliberate, calculated so the men would bond together against a common enemy—their drill sergeant? And if they hated passionately enough, feared the man enough, would they maybe pull together to avoid the sergeant's wrath?

Too bizarre, he decided. And yet the thought wouldn't go away.

Yes—maybe that was why he'd tried to encourage David Monroe. In civilian life, he'd have watched him suffer and felt good. Survival of the fittest. But this was the army. Like him or not, they were buddies. They had to work together and know they could depend on each other, no matter what.

"Now, watch again, Monroe," Carver said, trying to hide his exasperation. The guy was all thumbs. "You do it like this. Real easy." He smoothed the sheet on David's bed, folded a corner into a sharp crease and in one fluid movement, tucked it under the mattress.

"You gotta practice. You gotta get it down to two minutes if you wanna be out to PT in fifteen. Get it? You do it!" Carver yanked the sheet off the bed and passed it to David.

David despised himself for being so clumsy over something as elementary as making a bed. He resented being talked through this dumb procedure as if he were a mental retard. He resented Williams's obvious contempt. He flapped out the sheet with the force he'd have liked to apply to Williams's jaw.

It was the hour before lights-out, the only minutes in the long day for free time. Across the way several recruits were going through the Smart Book, drilling each other on the order of ranks. Two guys with towels wrapped around their middles headed for the shower. One guy was on the floor practicing sit-ups. A few trainees wrote letters, or clustered together, just talking.

"Not bad. Again!" Carver yawned as he ripped the sheet off the bed once more. "I'll time this one." He held up a stop watch. "Okay—go!"

"MAIL CALL!"

David's heart beat faster. He rushed to stand in the circle of eager trainees. Today, surely, there'd be *something.* He didn't know if he could stand the silence any longer. He needed a touch from home, some sign that out there were people who knew where he was and missed him.

He had no idea of what was going on in the outside world. They'd not been allowed a newspaper, not heard news on a radio; not seen a single TV show.

Every minute of every day was focused on getting in shape for the PT tests, and beyond that—the midcycle and end-of-cycle tests. He'd been totally isolated, deprived—of all the pleasures that normal life offered.

Even knowing it took most of a week for mail to come from California, each day he'd gone to mail call, hoping. He held his breath when the sergeant called out a name and flipped an envelope toward the trainee who answered. The guy from New Orleans who bunked below him had gotten mail. So had guys from New York and Oregon. Even Williams, who lived only a few miles from where he did, had gotten a letter. He'd seen his usually expressionless face light up as the letter was handed back, and then a brief look of joy as he recognized the name of the sender.

But for him there'd been nothing, not from Bree, not from Mom or even Heather.

"Anderson, Jason . . . Brown, Kevin . . . Fineman, Eric." Sergeant Baker sent letters flying over heads as they stood at parade rest.

"George, Andrew . . . Gregarian, Thomas . . ."

Almost to the M's. David shifted to see around the man in front, hands sweaty, a lump in his throat.

"I didn't know Baker could read . . ." someone beside David whispered, bringing on a twitter of laughter.

Sergeant Baker stopped calling names. Eyes narrowed, he glared at the men. "We have a comedian in the ranks? Which one's the wise guy?" His head swiveled slowly right to left.

Absolute silence. David's hands grew clammy. It was the New Yorker, two guys to his left, the one whose accent was so thick, he was hard to understand.

"I'm sorry, Drill Sergeant Baker," the soldier said. "Just kidding."

"You got K.P., soldier." Baker rolled a rubber band around the remaining envelopes. "Dis-missed!"

"What about our mail?" David called out. His pulse thumped wildly in his throat. How could Baker be so cruel? The very next letter might be *his* and here he was walking away!

"Tomorrow, soldier," Baker answered. "If you maggots learn a little discipline!"

"Fall in!" the platoon leader barked. "On the double!"

Head down, David trotted out behind the rest of the platoon to the exercise field. Another twenty-four hours of misery before the next mail call.

"Ouch!" he heard behind him.

"You frig up mail call again, Torres, and you're *dead*!" someone hissed.

And I'll be the one to kill you, David thought with savage satisfaction.

CHAPTER

10

"TEN-SHUN! Ready for inspection!"

David froze, then with wide-eyed terror shoved his footlocker under the bed and hurried to stand in the aisle. His boots looked good. He ran a nervous hand over his uniform and took a quick glance back to see if his bed would pass. The room smelled of boot polish and sweat.

"Yee! I'm not ready!" Brown exclaimed from nearby, a hysterical pitch to his voice. He slammed his locker shut. "Damn! I left my keys inside!"

Williams materialized from nowhere. He shook the locker door, called out for a screwdriver and tried to pick the lock, but failed. The inspection team, headed by the two platoon drill sergeants, started down the bay. Carver pushed Brown into the aisle and scurried into position at the side of the squad.

"Is *this* what you call making a bed, lady?" From the corner of his eye David saw a mattress from one of the other squads yanked off a bed and flung to the floor. "Down for ten, boy!"

"What's this f-in' footlocker doing here? Squad leader?"

"I don't know, Drill Sergeant!" a scared voice answered.

"You don't *know*? These scumbags are your responsibility, squad leader!" David heard the scrape of metal being kicked across the linoleum floor and tried to remember where his own locker had landed; not where it was supposed to be, he guessed.

"Fire guard duty, nine to midnight!"

The inspection team moved on, drawing closer. "Look at this! You slimebuckets, you vermin!" Sound of hangers being ripped off rods. A wastebasket being knocked over. David's heart banged against his ribs. Sweat poured down his sides. Soon Baker would come to him.

"Well . . . what have we *here*?" The drill sergeant's voice turned amazingly sweet and David's mouth went dry. For a second he thought he was addressing him, but no. It was O'Neill. The sergeant dangled a small, battery-operated radio from its strap, right in front of O'Neill's eyes.

Damn! Where'd that come from? David wondered. How'd O'Neill manage to hide it from the inspectors at the reception center? Now we're in for it.

"This yours, Private?"

"Yes, Drill Sergeant," O'Neill said.

"Is it, now? You didn't know, of course, that it's against regulations!"

"I couldn't see where it would matter, Sergeant Baker. I only listen after lights-out. I had a group, see? The Crap Shoots. Ever hear of them?"

A titter of laughter began but was quickly subdued by the look on Baker's face.

"Crap Shoot, huh? Isn't that fine," Baker said kindly. "I'll make a *crap shoot* of your ass, O'Neill! This is not a summer camp. How often do I have to say that? You are in the United States Army, boy! You are not here for fun! You are not here to listen to music after lights-out! *Do you understand*?" Sergeant Baker paused as if to let his words sink in. His scar turned a deep shade of red and his neck muscles grew rigid. "My job is to change you candy-assed civilians into soldiers! Is that clear?"

"Yes, Drill Sergeant Baker." O'Neill's voice trembled.

"Yes, Drill Sergeant Baker!" David echoed with the rest of the squad.

The sergeant jammed the small radio into a pocket. "Maggot! If you have enough energy to stay awake after lights-out, then maybe I'm not pushing you hard enough. Is that possible?"

"No, Sergeant!"

"Oh, I think so. I think you've had it too easy. Tell you what—how about you run around the track, after PT today. Say, ten times? Think that might tire you out?"

"Excuse me, Sergeant Baker. May I say something?"

"Certainly, maggot!"

"I—I think I made a mistake. I don't belong in the army. I want to go home."

"You do, do you?" A peculiar smile lit the sergeant's face. "You one of those mentals, lady? You need a trip to the psycho ward?" Baker stuck his face close to O'Neill's. "You a quitter, boy? *I say you can't quit*! Trainees under my command don't quit! What do you say to that?"

"But, but . . . I don't understand. This is a free country. I have a right to change my mind! I don't like the army. You won't let me smoke; I can't listen to a radio. I have to go to bed when you say. It's not democratic!" O'Neill's voice rose. "I'm . . . I'm . . . *unable to adapt*! It's in the rule book!" he finished, triumphant.

"A week in the army and you're unable to adapt? I'll pretend I didn't hear that. *Boy*—you're soft as a marshmallow. You *need* the army, and the army's gonna make you into a *man*. You want to quit? Not today. See me in two weeks, then I'll decide. Meanwhile, *you get out there on the exercise field with the rest of your platoon*! Do you understand?" He turned away. "Squad leader?"

"Sergeant?" Carver answered.

"Have your squad on the field in five minutes!"

Passing David, Sergeant Baker moved on. His voice rang out as he zeroed in on other trainees. And then, finally, inspection was over.

Funny, Carver thought. If he'd have guessed who'd want out from his squad, he'd have picked anyone except O'Neill. Brown, maybe, because the sergeant picked on him so much and the strain showed. The kid had guts, but he wasn't built for all the physical stuff the army required. Yesterday he'd caught him crying, sitting on the floor with his back against a wall, running the water in the shower so no one would hear.

He figured that next to Brown, Monroe was the likeliest to want out. Sergeant picked on him, too, but for different reasons. Monroe didn't put out a hundred percent. He had an *attitude*. Kind of—above it all, and why not? Monroe could leave anytime he wanted. He had a lot to fall back on, coming from rich folks like he did.

But—O'Neill? He'd figured him for something of a hell-raiser. Everything was a joke with him. Still, the guy had spirit. Maybe that kind was the hardest to tame. He'd have to talk to O'Neill. Didn't he realize he could get through all this if he just understood one thing? That all you had to do was play the game? "Yes Sarge" them or "No Sarge" them like you meant what you said? And it didn't mean diddly-squat?

"Squad—fall in," Carver called, leading the way out to the exercise field behind the three other squads.

He felt a pull in his gut when he saw the guidon, the forked flag carried by one member of the platoon during all marches or runs. It was furled. Rolled and tied on its staff. A sign of shame. A sign to the whole world that the thirty-eight men of second platoon had fouled up. Because they hadn't cleaned their barracks to standards in the time allotted. And it would stay furled until they met regulations.

"My buddy's in a foxhole, with a bullet in his head!" Sergeant Baker sang out, and the platoon repeated as they moved out at double time.

"I'm wondering in my mind if he's really dead. . . ."

Moving briskly, Carver echoed the line.

"I hear the choppers coming. They're hovering overhead. . . .

"They come to get the wounded. They come to get the dead. . . ."

Carver sang the cadence again, and a third time, trotting along with his platoon. And suddenly he thought, Yeah! This is what it's all about. . . . This is why they push us so hard! A funny twang of excitement rushed down his arms and legs.

PAULA stood at arm's length behind Tania as the line into the mess hall moved slowly, but steadily. It was the end of the day. After dinner there'd be two more hours of classroom study and then, joy of joys—a chance to shower and relax before lights out.

"Oh, oh," Tania whispered. "Brunhilda's at the door, holding up cards or something. I can't see . . ."

"She's testing us!" Christine exclaimed. "Oh, God!"

"Just keep cool." Paula tried to see around Tania to where Sergeant Thompson—Brunhilda, they called her behind her back—stood at the door to the mess hall. She could barely make out a white card with a picture of lieutenant's bars. "It's what we've been learning from the Smart Book. You won't have any trouble." She hoped her words would sound reassuring.

"I will! I will! I'm hopeless at remembering!" Christine cried. Her ivory skin flamed pink. "Oh, what am I going to do? It all flies out of my head as soon as she looks at me!"

In the few days they'd been together the three of them had drawn close. An unlikely trio, Paula thought. A black girl from Chicago, a white single mother, and her. Tania had skin as dark as midnight, and a kind of street smarts and openness that Paula found refreshing. And Christine, so pink and blond and innocent, despite her amazing sexual history, seemed terribly vulnerable.

"Pray," Tania whispered as they drew closer to the drill sergeant. "Pray you'll get an easy one. Dear God . . ."

"What's CO mean?" Thompson threw at Tania.

"Commanding officer!"

Lucky Tania. An easy one, Paula thought.

Tania moved on into the mess hall and it was Paula's turn. "No haircut yet, Carlson?" The drill sergeant's lips curled into a smile, but the eyes remained cold.

"No, Drill Sergeant!" She's not really a bad-looking woman, Paula thought, if only she'd let her hair grow and use a little eye makeup. Thompson sniffed the air so her thin nose wrinkled. "Order of rank!"

Paula closed her eyes for an instant. She could see the words on the page of the Smart Book in her head. "Order of rank: general—four stars," she said. "Major general, three. No!" she immediately corrected. "*Lieutenant general* with three! *Then* major general!"

"Make up your mind! Which is it?" Thompson challenged, as if hoping she'd make a mistake.

"Lieutenant general—three stars; major general *two*. . . ." She went on to call off the remaining ranks and insignia without error. Thompson waved her through with an impatient flourish of a hand.

Paula took a deep, relieved breath and realized her legs were shaking. It wasn't the classroom knowledge that she found hard. She knew how to cram. And most of the stuff didn't take any deep intelligence: how to salute, and who, and under what circumstances. That sort of thing.

She was as sore as everyone else from all the exercise, but that would pass in time. What she found hardest was the lack of privacy. She'd always had her own room. Because of work and school, she'd had no time for friendships. Dan had been her only social outlet for months. And now, suddenly, she was surrounded by people. And while she liked many of the women, she missed the chance to think. Even driving the freeways, rushing from school to job, or home —her mind had been free. Not here. Only at night, in bed, was there time to think. She worried about her mother, alone for the first time since her father died. And she thought about Dan. But usually she was so tired, she fell asleep as soon as her head touched the pillow.

Paula carried her tray with meat loaf, cole slaw, a mound of mashed potatoes and a limp stalk of broccoli to a table where the rest of her squad sat.

For a moment she held her fork over the food, imagining a big California salad with shrimp or crabmeat and lots of fresh veggies. That's what she'd want on a hot, humid day like today, not this. But her appetite surprised her. She ate enormous breakfasts and whatever was served at other meals. She downed everything and even so, suspected she'd lost weight.

"Some guy's looking at you, Paula," Christine said, nudging her arm. "Good-lookin' too . . ."

"Where?"

Christine pointed with a fork.

"Oh!" Paula's eyes locked on David. He sat at a nearby table watching her. He looked thinner than she remembered from a week ago, and haggard. She wondered what he thought about the army now. He smiled and held her gaze until she felt warmth creep into her heart and a responsive grin on her lips. Then, angry with herself for feeling what she promised herself not to allow again—she looked away.

CHAPTER

11

☆

CARVER PATTED HIS SHIRT POCKET where Lavonne's last letter lay close to his heart. He carried the letter wherever he went. It comforted him, made all the strangeness and loneliness of being in this place a bit more bearable.

The guys pulled out photos of their girls whenever there was time for talk, and boasted about their conquests. He knew about O'Neill's Kathy and Telemantes's Carmelita. He'd seen a picture of Monroe's girl, too. She had a snooty name, like an expensive cheese—Bree. And she looked like what you'd expect Monroe to go for—the pep squad type he'd seen at the La Cañada football games—tall, pretty, and blond.

When it was his turn to boast, he'd said nothing about Lavonne. That was his business, to be shared with nobody, nohow! Instead, to satisfy their curiosity, he'd invented some raunchy stories that left the guys openmouthed and bug-eyed.

"Carver dear," Lavonne's letter began. He memorized the words and read them over in his head again and again. "The days are so sad without you, so long and empty."

Yes, he'd thought, *Yes. Even here, where they keep you busy every minute, I miss you like crazy.*

"I make the lunches and get the kids off to school every morning, just like always. Wake Mom, and leave. No Carver to walk me to school, to see between classes, to eat lunch with. No Carver to see after work, to talk with, to love. How will I stand it, being apart—for three whole years?"

Carver had held the letter close to his cheek for a long moment, infusing himself with Lavonne's spirit. *Yes, sweet Lavonne, yes,* he'd said to himself. *I know.*

She had written the news of the neighborhood, about her best friend applying for a college scholarship, about a kid they knew who got picked up for dealing. *About seeing Kisha with Deon in his new white Mercedes!*

The day the letter arrived he could think of little else except what Lavonne had said about Kisha. The worry made him sick inside. He was short with anyone who spoke to him and even considered chucking it all, going AWOL. He could hardly wait until the free hour before lights-out. He'd phone, at least, and find out what was going on. F the regulations. If he was caught—he'd pay the consequences.

"Kisha?" It was his sister who answered.

"Carver? Mom! Come quick! It's Carver!"

"Wait! I want to talk with *you.* How are you, honeybun? How's it going?"

"Fine. I miss you! It's lonesome without you here. . . ."

Was she hiding something? Did he hear a guarded tone? In a moment his mother would take over and then he couldn't find out. "Lavonne wrote that she saw you in Deon's car," he said, coming straight to the point. "That true?"

She hesitated long enough for him to sense the guilt. "He only picked me up after school . . . for a little ride."

"Listen, honeybun!" he said intently. "You stay away from Deon. Far away! He's *bad* news! Jeez, Kisha! You promised you wouldn't go *anywhere* with him. You know the score. You promised! You said you'd even go to a friend's place, like I told you, if Mom's out and you're alone with him! I thought I could trust you!"

He heard Kisha's intake of breath, could almost see the stubborn pout that always came to her face when scolded. He was taking a chance. She liked to think she was all grown up and could care for herself, but there was no time for diplomacy now. Not with Baker likely to descend on him any time. "Understand?" he repeated in a more strident tone than before.

"I'm not a baby anymore! I can take care of myself!" Kisha cried.

"Sure, like Ma who got pregnant with me at your age!"

"Let me speak to him! Kisha, give me the phone!" his mother said in the background.

"Honeybun?" he persisted. "I want your promise! Stay away from that shit! Don't believe a thing he says. Now put Mom on. Don't forget. Love ya."

And then his mother spoke. "How you doin', honey?" she asked, and before he could answer, bubbled, "We're all making plans to come out for your graduation. Kisha and me. Even Lavonne, but it's supposed to be a surprise. Deon's getting tickets. . . ."

The spurt of pleasure he felt at hearing he might see Lavonne in seven more weeks nearly made him forget why he phoned. But knowing that Baker might come by any time squelched the momentary joy. "Mom . . . Mom! Hold it!" he almost shouted as she babbled on without pause. "Listen. I haven't much time. *I don't want Deon hanging around Kisha.* Hear? Tell him to stay away, a *mile* away! Tell him—if he doesn't, next time I see him I'll *cut off his balls!*"

"Car-ver, honey! What you talking 'bout?"

"You *know* what I'm talking about, Ma. Don't close your eyes just 'cause you don't want to see. I told you before he's been eyeballin' Kisha, so you watch him! Hear?" He turned from the phone as he heard voices. "Listen. Gotta go. Take care. And don't forget what I said!"

He was glad he'd phoned, though he wasn't sure what good it would do. Maybe, at least, Kisha would be more careful. He scurried back to barracks, adjusting his face to the bland expression he wore around the guys. Baker wasn't around. The others were busy with chores. Only Monroe glanced up, a look of curiosity on his face.

"REPEAT AFTER ME," Sergeant Baker ordered, holding high the M-16 that he had just stripped and put back together for the benefit of the platoon. "This is my rifle. My rifle is my best friend. There are many like it, but this one is mine."

They were in a classroom, getting instruction in rifle maintenance. David ran a hand over the barrel of the rifle, feeling its cold, smooth steel. It reminded him of the BB gun he'd owned briefly, which he'd got from his *real* father for his eighth birthday. His mother had been furious. It had led to a terrible fight between his parents. But in the end, his father had won.

The day he'd gone up in the hills to learn how to shoot he'd felt more than a little scared, but also very proud. He owned a gun, the only kid in the neighborhood!

"Just remember," his father had repeated again and again. "This is not a toy. You could hurt someone with it. It's okay to shoot at targets, but never at living things. And before you ever pull that trigger, you make darn sure there's no one in the way."

And now he was holding an M-16. It could fire a single round or as many as 940 rounds a minute! One burst could tear a man into nine hundred little pieces. For a moment that realization stunned him. The M-16 was not just a toy, and not just for target practice. It was for *killing*. For killing guys his own age—guys he didn't know, would never know, guys who loved their wives or sweethearts, their mothers and fathers. Guys his government said he had to kill, because they were the *enemy*.

"THIS is your *rifle*." Sergeant Baker held up the M-16. "And this is your gun." He placed a hand over the bulge in his pants. "This is for killing." Again, he held up his rifle. "And this is for fun."

David grinned. The meaning was all too clear.

"Now, repeat after me . . ." Baker continued. "I must fire my rifle true. I must shoot straighter than the enemy of my country who may be trying to shoot at me. My rifle and I are a team. Together we are defenders of my country . . . and are dedicated to its defense unto death. Before God, I swear this!"

". . . Before God, I swear this . . ." the platoon repeated.

"Now . . ." Baker said, after a pause to let the words sink in, "Let us strip the M-16. We will take it apart piece by piece and put it together again. First —remove the magazine. . . ."

"Not like that, you friggin' idiot!" Baker shouted when they got to dismantling the bolt carrier assembly. David shuddered as the sergeant strode toward him with a murderous gleam in his eyes. His hands fumbled with the cocking handle, and his elbow nearly knocked the magazine to the floor. "Good God, Monroe! Where *were* you when the Lord passed out brains? I said, 'slide it to the rear,' not the front!" He grabbed David's rifle and showed him what he meant, then thrust it back into his hands. "Now—do it again!"

He's a maniac. A sadist, David thought as he struggled to strip the rifle while Baker stood over him. Christ, he knew how to do it! He'd owned his own gun, hadn't he? He was as mechanical as the next guy, maybe more so, and in more than fair physical shape. But not around Drill Sergeant Baker. Every time the man so much as glanced his way, David's brain turned to mush and he did all the wrong things. Maybe *he* should have said *I quit*, not O'Neill, because he sure couldn't see six more weeks of this shit and coming out sane or alive!

If only he'd heard from Bree! How could she not write? He felt as if he'd dropped out of the world and no one cared. Well, maybe someone. Heather did. His kid sister had written twice, on purple, lined paper, filling each page with big, rounded letters. And his mother had written about a trip to Hawaii she'd be taking with Charlie and how they missed having him around. *Sure.* But from Bree—nothing.

"All right. Now do it again, and *faster!*" Baker said, moving on. "You guys are gonna do this again, and again, until you can do it with your eyes shut. Nothing. I repeat—*nothing*—is as important as your M-16!"

"EVER HANDLE A RIFLE BEFORE?" Paula asked Christine as they clung to the truck's wood bench seats. It had rained, briefly, and her shirt stuck to her skin, but the rain had not come down long enough to soak the washboard-rutted dirt road that led to the firing range. As a result, each truck kicked up a tail of dust that hung in the still air for those behind to inhale.

In the morning they had done the usual exercises, then, carrying their M-16s, had marched double time for two miles. They had learned to transfer the weapon on command, from right to left, from left to right, and to clean it and put it together in minutes. Today, for the first time, they would actually fire the M-16s against a target.

"Handle a rifle?" Christine chuckled. "Can't remember when I didn't. Used to hunt raccoons with

Daddy and my brothers. Sure, I know somethin'. You?"

"Never *saw* a gun till this week, much less held one."

"*Rifle* . . ." Christine corrected her. "Don't let Brunhilda hear you call it a gun." She peered anxiously into Paula's face and put a hand on her arm. "Why, honey! You're not *scared*, are you? Hey! There's nothin' to it."

Paula shrugged, embarrassed. She wasn't used to admitting weakness to anyone. Not even to Dan, whom she'd trusted for so long. Too long. Her mother had always said, "It's not smart telling people your faults. They can use it against you. Just show them your good side." And here she was showing her vulnerability to a total stranger, a girl who looked sixteen, had the experience of a thirty-year-old, yet remained as open and guileless as an eight-year-old.

"I can't imagine killing someone."

"Aw. Nothin' to it," Christine exclaimed. "I killed lots a' things. Birds, raccoons . . . Aim right and they never feel a thing."

"Besides," Tania chimed in, "we don't gotta do the killing. That's for the guys. All *we* gotta do is shoot back if we're surrounded by the enemy."

"Talkin' of the enemy—look who's here!"

A truck filled with male trainees returning from the firing range rumbled by, kicking up a cloud of dust.

"Guys!"

"Ooohee!" Christine craned her neck for a better look.

"Ain't you had enough trouble, girl?" Tania asked.

"I ain't *never* gonna have enough! No, ma'am." Christine laughed. "How 'bout you, Paula?"

"I've sworn off. They're nothing but pain," Paula said, grinning.

"Ooohee. That's for sure," Christine agreed. "But such *sweet* pain! Ooohee! You don't know half what you're missin'!"

CHAPTER

12

strove on, with everyone screaming while
the sergeant screamed for blood until his eyes. If
on our volunteered, Baker would choose opponents,
so I did had no desire to be one of them.

IT WAS THE END of the second week. David
had to admit he felt good. The muscles that had cried
for mercy the first days of basic barely gave him a
twinge now. His abdomen was as hard and flat as
marble. He could run two miles and hardly puff. His
head was crammed with facts about first aid, map
reading—and much more.

What hadn't changed was his fear and hate of the
drill sergeant. He'd awake late at night from his own
agonized mutterings, dreaming that he and Baker
were going at each other in hand-to-hand combat.
His fists would be clenched. His teeth would hurt
from grinding them, and his cheeks would be wet.
He'd lie in bed breathing hard, and wondering what
he'd really do to Baker if he ever got the chance.

"Okay, you turds," the sergeant had said yesterday. "Time to bash each other's head in." He'd

drawn a large circle with the toe of a boot and held up two pugil sticks. "Volunteers?"

Standing with the rest of his platoon around the circle's outer rim, David had assumed a look of anonymity. The long sticks were padded at each end but had the punch power of boxing gloves. The object was to knock the opponent out of the circle with any blow above the belt. He'd fought in group practice, but not one-to-one with everyone watching while the sergeant screamed for blood from the sidelines. If no one volunteered, Baker would choose opponents, and David had no desire to be one of them.

"No volunteers? No? You ladies afraid you'll break your fingernails?" Baker asked sweetly. He stood in the middle of the circle, eyeballing each of them. David stared straight ahead.

"Brown—how about you?" The sergeant's gaze traveled around the circle, paused on David, then moved on. "And you—O'Neill . . ."

David let out his breath. *Brown and O'Neill.* What unfair pairing. Brown weighed thirty pounds less than O'Neill. The sergeant knew the kid tried harder than anyone else but lacked stamina and strength. O'Neill had both strength and stamina, but lacked discipline and considered the whole army experience a big joke. "Bug off," he'd said when David, on fire guard duty one night, caught him smoking.

"Okay, scumbags. Let's go!" the sergeant had barked, tossing each man one of the pugil sticks. "And I don't want any pussyfooting! This is *war* you're preparing for. You're *enemies.* It's *your* life or his!"

The sergeant fingered the whistle hanging from a lanyard around his neck, lifted it to his lips, and blew.

The two men moved toward each other in the center of the circle, wielding the stick with both hands. "Come on, Brown, come on," O'Neill teased softly. "You're gonna be mincemeat before I'm through!" He stalked Brown like a prizefighter sizing up his opponent, a confident smile on his lips.

Suddenly, O'Neill swung his pugil stick in a wicked blow to Brown's shoulder. A look of surprise and pain flashed across the kid's face.

"Give it to him!" some of the guys in the platoon shouted. "Get him! Kill! Kill!"

"The little guy's *dead*!"

"What's he just standin' there for? Hey, kid! Fight!"

David clenched his teeth and strained across the line toward Brown. So far the kid had taken half a dozen hard blows. His nose bled and a cut had opened on one cheek. He swung his stick mostly in defense. Why didn't he strike back? What was wrong with him?

"Come on, Brown! Come on! Give it to him!" David called, punching the air with angry fists.

"The kid's chicken," the guy beside him said. "Bet you five O'Neill flattens 'im."

"You're on," David said, not taking his eyes from the circle.

"Fight, damn you, lady!" Baker roared. "I want blood! Clobber him!"

Suddenly, pushed almost to the edge of the circle, Brown made his move. In one quick thrust he jabbed the pugil stick into O'Neill's solar plexus. Taking advantage of the shock and pain he pounded away at every opening until O'Neill fell back. Then, moving swiftly around O'Neill, he forced him to turn so *he* was now backed against the circle's rim.

"Get 'im!" David yelled. "Kill 'im!" He felt a surge of exhilaration. What Brown lacked in physical strength he more than made up in smarts and guts, David thought. Look how he ignored the pain. Look how he watched O'Neill, waiting for just the right moment to take advantage.

No longer smiling, O'Neill staggered, then regained balance. Furious now, he lunged at Brown, wielding the pugil stick like a club, sometimes as a bayonet, thrusting, battering, jabbing, while the thirty-six men around the outside of the circle screamed encouragement.

"I'll take the five," the man beside David said, holding out a hand, eyes still on the opponents.

"Not yet you don't!" David replied as Brown danced out of reach while maneuvering O'Neill toward the circle's rim. Then, with one quick and sudden thrust, followed by a killing shower of hammer blows, he knocked his opponent over the line.

"No fair!" O'Neill raged, leaping back into the circle.

Baker blew the whistle, once and twice more as O'Neill refused to yield. "Game's over, soldier!"

Brown, lips swollen and a dark bruise on one cheek, let out a wild, victorious yell and waved his stick high overhead. Wiping the sweat from his brow and the blood from his nose, O'Neill threw the pugil stick to the ground and stalked off.

"Told ya." David punched the arm of the soldier beside him. "I'll take that five." O'Neill should have quit two weeks ago when he wanted out, David thought. He'd never make it through basic, with his attitude. More often than not it was *his* bunk or locker that didn't measure up so the whole squad suffered. If it hadn't been for his being caught smoking again, their platoon wouldn't have had to do a two-mile full-pack run with flag furled.

Some of the guys had already lost patience. The men talked privately about how to get back at O'Neill, how to teach him a lesson so he'd shape up, especially since his last prank. He had stashed smokes and candy in a hole he'd dug behind a recruiting poster. Baker had found it. Instead of punishing O'Neill, the drill sergeant had made the whole platoon do sit-ups while O'Neill was told to stand at ease and call the count.

Now, jogging beside his buddies to an instruction class, David smiled to himself. O'Neill deserved what he got.

"Hey, man," he heard someone behind him whisper. "How come you let a runt like Brown flatten you?"

"Aw, shut up . . ." O'Neill muttered.

"How you gonna make it out in the jungles if you can't even hold your own against a midget?"

"Go to hell!"

David glanced sideways, saw O'Neill's neck getting redder, a sure sign that his short fuse was burning low.

"Standin' tall, lookin' good . . ." Baker sang out, jogging along beside the platoon, face turned toward them.

"Oughta—be—in Hollywood . . ."

David stole another look at O'Neill. The red in his neck subsided as he took up the cadence with the rest of the platoon. Had Baker seen the trouble and averted it? How much could O'Neill take?

"ALL RIGHT! I've had enough of you guys!" O'Neill shouted later when they were back in their barracks. The platoon had buzzed around him like fleas, rubbing it in that he'd lost to the smallest guy in the platoon. David had seen the outburst coming. O'Neill's face flamed red again. He'd roughly elbowed guys crowding him and shoved one man to the floor before two guys grabbed him.

"That's enough!" Williams had shouted. "You'll have the drill sergeants down on all of us!"

"Shit! I'm not gonna put up with this crap! Brown threw a lucky punch, that's all!" O'Neill cried, struggling free.

"Oh, sure. Lucky punch! Quit, O'Neill, like you shoulda two weeks ago. Can't depend on you, nohow, so you may as well. Good riddance, too!"

"Make me!" O'Neill broke through the wall of men and turned to face them, legs apart, fists bared.

"Put your money where your mouth is," someone shouted.

"Nobody *makes* me quit. I go *if* and *when* I want. You guys want me out? Here's the deal. One of you beats me at push-ups—I'm out!" O'Neill's eyes swept the room, challenging, confident. No one in the platoon had suffered as much floor time with sit-ups and push-ups as he. "Who'll take me on?"

David levered himself off the bed where he was studying the Smart Book. This could be interesting. O'Neill had his back to the wall. Strong and determined, that fighting spirit was focused now. He couldn't stand another defeat in front of the whole platoon, but who'd take him on? The only one possible was Williams. He still led the platoon in PT, climbing ropes and ladders faster than anyone, crawling through dirt and mud in the best time, outlasting them all at sit-ups and push-ups.

"You guys chicken? Afraid I'll beat you?" O'Neill laughed humorlessly. "Nobody? Then *lay off*. I'll do what I want. And if you slimes don't like it, go to hell!"

"I'll take you on, smartass." Williams had moved to the center of the room. "But if I win—you *stay* and you *shape up* 'cause we're all powerful sick of paying for the trouble you cause."

"Go to hell!"

Williams peeled off his shirt, tossed it on a bed, then dropped to the floor. "Let's go, O'Neill."

"You're on."

"Bets anyone? What odds will you give me? Williams or O'Neill?" Telemantes pulled a pad out of his footlocker, licked the end of a pencil, and stood poised to take bets.

Recruits clustered on beds, crowded the aisles, peered around as O'Neill dropped beside Carver and held himself in the front-lean and rest position.

"Go!" someone yelled.

The count began. "One, two, three, four . . . Sixteen, seventeen, eighteen . . . Thirty-three, thirty-four . . . Forty-one . . . Fifty-nine, sixty . . ."

"Go! Go! *Williams*," David shouted, though he couldn't understand why. He disliked the dude plain and simple, not the least of why being Williams's obvious dislike of him. And it had nothing to do with color. He'd had black friends before they moved to La Cañada.

What would Williams be thinking now? he wondered. *Can't let a white guy beat me?* Was that what it was all about? His dark skin glistened. David could hear his sharp intakes of breath. "Sixty-three. Sixty-four. Sixty-five." To win he'd have to go five more than O'Neill, whose face was red as an apple now, but who had the glazed eyes of someone in a trance.

"Sixty-eight. Sixty-nine . . ."

Both men were drawing ragged breaths. Sweat dripped from their faces and heads. Williams's arms showed a tremor in the raised position.

"Two bucks on Williams! Hell, no. Give you five for O'Neill . . ."

"Seventy. Seventy-one!"

He's not gonna make it, David thought when he saw the agonized expression on Williams's usually expressionless face. He seemed to be favoring his left arm. David felt a grudging admiration, knowing the pain he must be enduring.

"Seventy-three. Seventy-four!" the voices chanted in unison.

A sigh of disappointment went through the room as Williams suddenly paused, arms quivering in the front-lean and rest position, then collapsed. He lay heaving, one cheek against the floor while the count went on.

"Eighty-four! Eighty-five!" the men in the platoon roared. "Eighty-six!"

O'Neill's fair skin had turned as red as raw meat. A wheezy scream came from his chest. "Ninety . . . ninety-one!" Suddenly, with a great release of breath, he passed out.

"Give him air! Get water!"

One of the recruits rushed up and doused half a

bucket of water over O'Neill, soaking Williams as well. Williams staggered to his feet and leaned against the nearest bed.

"Someone get the medics!" Brown called just as O'Neill sputtered back to life. "Nah . . . he'll be okay. Better clean this mess before Baker catches us."

Y'ass belongs to me, Baker had bawled during one of the excruciating PT sessions when he'd had them doing endless push-ups in the hot sun on pavement that burned their palms. David thought of Baker's words as he went for a mop. *Y'ass belongs to me and only incidentally to the U.S. Army! And when I'm through with it, y'all gonna be soldiers!*

Maybe the drill sergeant, as mean as he was, knew what he was doing after all, he thought. Not that that excused his heartless behavior. But two weeks ago who'd have thought O'Neill would stick it out, would push himself till he passed out? Maybe the guy was taking the army seriously at last. Maybe he'd make a soldier yet.

CHAPTER

13

"YAH! YAH! KILL!" the platoon around Paula screamed as they ran toward the building where they'd see yet another training film. Such a stupid order! Yet she had obeyed it because Drill Sergeant Thompson, Brunhilda, had stared directly at her when she'd given the instructions, as if only she might object.

In off moments, Paula tried to understand the psychology of descending on a classroom like a horde of savages attacking a fort but had decided it was just another of those orders you had to follow, whether or not they made sense.

Now, as she ran forward with the rest, screaming, she thought—maybe it's to keep our minds occupied so we haven't time to think. And in that instant when her brain took over, she resented being pressed into a mold identical with everyone else. As hard as it had been at home, working and going to school, she'd had her own space and time. Here, for these last two weeks, she'd become a robot whose mechanisms were manipulated by others.

"Kill! Yah! Yah! Kill!"

"Peace!" Paula called out, suppressing an urge to giggle. When no one near her reacted, caught up in their own mindless repetitions, she shouted a bit louder. "Peace!"

"Paula!" the girl beside her whispered without turning her head. "She'll murder you!"

Sergeant Thompson waited at the doorway, checking her platoon as they filed by into the classroom. Paula bit her lip to stifle a grin. She wondered if the woman ever sweated, ever creased her uniform, ever spoke in less than a rasping growl. She couldn't imagine Thompson cuddling a baby, or in bed with a man . . . unless she was the aggressor.

Whether she gave her thoughts away by the expression on her face or Thompson had pegged her as someone to break, she didn't know. But the sergeant stopped the flow of soldiers into the classroom just as Paula approached the door.

"Carlson!"

Here we go again, Paula thought. She came to attention and saluted, looking directly into the drill sergeant's eyes. "Yes, Sergeant!"

"Name the reasons and order for chaptering out!"

A tingle of fear rushed through Paula's veins. Why that particular question? Was Brunhilda trying to remind her that she might not make it? She knew the reasons for being dismissed from the army—drug involvement, failure to pass physical tests, inability to adjust, *attitude*. . . . That was the one they could get her on. Because, no matter how Brunhilda tried to break her, Paula had kept part of herself free.

"Chapter one . . ." she began, trembling inside, mind racing ahead to sort out the answers.

By the time she had finished, Thompson's steel-eyed gaze had changed to hate. The drill sergeant could not make an example of her, could not ridicule her in front of the others. Had to wave her on.

Paula moved on by and took a seat on a bench in the first row. "Phew. She's really got it in for you," Christine whispered.

"Yeah. Hasn't gotten over Paula's not cutting her hair."

"Carlson!"

The tingle of fear was back. Paula turned quickly to see Sergeant Thompson glaring down at her.

"You better uncross your legs, Private, or I'll knock you flat on the floor!"

Blood rushed to Paula's face. She uncrossed her legs and stared straight ahead. Thompson moved to the front of the room.

"Today you will be seeing three films. The first is on good dental procedures—how to brush and floss."

"R rated, no doubt," someone behind Paula whispered.

"The second will be on obedience . . ."

Joining the army was the biggest mistake of my life, Paula thought, eyes glazing over.

"And the third—and most important—film you will see is on how to put on and maintain your 'protective masks.' " The sergeant's face broke into what appeared to be a smile. "Next week you will learn about protective masks firsthand. You will don your masks, go into the gas chamber, and when the gas is on you will remove those masks, say your name, rank, and serial number—before you are released."

"Ugh . . ." Tania whispered. "They're trying to kill us."

"You will learn—from this experience—the *importance* of wearing your masks in the event of chemical warfare." Thompson rested her eyes on Paula for an instant. Then, with unaccustomed delight, she tried to make a joke. "Not to worry, ladies. It's been three weeks since we lost the last soldier to poison gas."

"BUS TO CHURCH leaves in ten minutes!" the voice over the loudspeaker announced. "Line up outside!"

"Aren't you coming?" Paula asked Christine. She had looked forward to Sunday church service not because she was religious, which she was not, but for the joy of escaping army life for a few hours. They'd be going to a church in town because the camp chapel was being painted. Town! She'd see civilians again. Families. Children!

"Go to church?" Christine answered from the cot where she lay on her stomach studying the latest pictures of her baby sent from home. "Why? I don't believe in God. Not since my mama died no matter how hard I prayed. And not after the Lord didn't stop my boyfriend from taking a walk when he heard I was pregnant. You believe that stuff?"

Paula smiled. "I'm going—to pray I'll survive the gas chamber." She took one last look in the small mirror on her locker and frowned. Normally, her skin was one of her best features—clear and creamy

—but look at it! All those freckles from so much sun! "I look like a *leopard*!" she lamented.

"Oh . . . you don't. Really," Christine said, checking her over critically. "You look nice. Wholesome, kinda. Like the girls guys take home to mama."

"Well, no guy's gonna take me home to mama. Not for a long time, a verrry long time." She pushed a loose strand of hair under her cap and turned around. "I'll help you memorize that M-16 stuff as soon as I get back."

DAVID filed into the church pew behind a dozen other trainees and took a seat on the end, next to the middle aisle. The ride in had been fun.

"You never been to New York?" one of the guys from Brooklyn had asked in astonishment when a kid from Tennessee wanted to know what it was like to ride in the subway. "Hey, Tony! You tell 'im."

"It's like this. Ya stand at the station waitin' for a train wid a zillion other guys. Ya see the train comin' down this dark tunnel, and already guys are pushin' and shovin'. . . . The doors open and ya push and shove like the rest. Don' matter who's in the way. You'd flatten your own motha'. You packed in so tight, ya can't tell which pervert is goosin' ya."

"Oooee!" the Tennessean exclaimed. "Ya gotta be crazy, livin' like *that*!"

The two New Yorkers laughed. "So, who says we ain't?"

They'd talked about going to church, and what religion meant, and his mind went back not to the last time he'd gone, when Mom and Charlie got married, but to an earlier time.

Mom had been pregnant with Heather. He'd just

learned about sex and remembered feeling funny about walking beside her because of her big belly.

"The family that prays together, stays together," Mom had said, sending Dad a meaningful glance. "Hogwash," his father had answered.

That day at church had been the last they'd gone anywhere as a family. Sitting between his parents, he'd felt an uneasy mix of comfort at their nearness and insecurity at their open hostility.

Now David sat quietly, hands folded over his army cap, letting the organ music wash over him, the serenity of the church fill him. He was glad he'd decided to come. He needed this island of quiet to do some serious thinking. Like maybe he *should* quit. There were six more weeks of this shit and all kinds of tests to take yet. Several guys from the company had chaptered out. It was rumored that one of the men had told his drill sergeant, "Don't try to stop me, 'cause if you do, better watch out when we're on the firing range!"

He hadn't realized how lonely it would be. He missed Heather's happy chatter, hanging around the kitchen nibbling and chatting with his mother before dinner, even Charlie and his know-it-all nagging. Surrounded by men twenty-four hours a day, programmed from early morning until late at night, he missed the easiness, the warmth of civilian life.

And Bree.

Except for one brief and impersonal letter, he'd heard nothing. He knew at least two guys who'd probably made a move on her as soon as he left. He'd made no promises, and neither had she. Maybe you couldn't expect a girl to wait two years.

"Chicks!" the guy from Brooklyn hissed, nudging his arm and nodding to the back of the church.

Two by two the female trainees filed by, taking seats across the aisle. One of the privates, a blonde, turned back to check them over, then leaned over to whisper something to the soldier beside her.

Is that her? David wondered with a shock of pleasure. He craned his neck, trying to see the profile of the only redhead in the row. Could it be? Yes! It *was* Paula! His depression lifted instantly. Maybe there'd be a social, after services. Maybe they'd have a chance to speak!

The organ music rose to a crescendo, then faded to silence as the minister approached the pulpit. The minister's eyes swept the congregation—half military, half civilian, then bent his head. "Let us pray." David reached for his prayer book.

"OH, MAN," one of the girls beside Paula exclaimed after the service. "Just look at that spread! I'm gonna pig out!"

A beautiful flower arrangement sat in the center of a table laden with an array of cakes and cookies, finger sandwiches and candies. Smiling women sat at each end of the table serving coffee and tea in china cups and saucers. Parents with small children dressed in Sunday best clustered around, swatting little hands grabbing for sweets, chatting with friends.

Paula reached for a cup of tea and smiled. "Thanks," she said. "It's kind of you all to let us share your church."

"You're welcome, dear," the woman answered.

Gloria D. Miklowitz

"God is for everyone. Besides, we're very proud to host you brave, unselfish young people."

"Yes, indeed," an elderly man added. "It's good young'uns like you defend our freedom."

Embarrassed, she moved on down the table checking out the food. She placed a couple of open-faced sandwiches and a pecan-studded honeybun on a plate, then eased through the crowd in search of her friends.

"Paula!"

Peering between heads was the young man from the plane—David Monroe. She felt a quickening of her pulse as his face broke into a warm grin. Thinner, he looked more like a man now than the too eager boy with the thick mane of sun-gold hair that she remembered.

In a moment he pushed his way by others and appeared in front of her, cap in hand. "Hey, it's good to see you! How's it going?"

Someone behind Paula jogged an elbow. "Oh!" she exclaimed as hot tea spilled over her.

"Are you okay? Here! Let me take that!" David relieved her of the teacup and plate. "Let's get out of here and see what we can do. Excuse me . . . excuse me . . ." He plowed through the crowd to a hall near the church offices and deposited Paula's teacup and edibles on a bench, then swung around. "Now, let's see that." He took her hand before she could stop him. "That burn looks mean. Let's see if we can find something for it."

"Now just a minute!" She pulled her hand out of his grasp, furious for letting him take over, for allowing him such familiarity. "Look. Thanks, but it's

(108)

nothing. After these last two weeks what's a little burn?" Two children ran down the hall, their voices echoing as they called to each other. "We better get back. I'm in enough trouble already with my drill sergeant."

"Stay a minute, please." His eyes pleaded with her. "The army's got us all week. It's Sunday. The devil's day off. Stay. You don't know what a pleasure it is to see you! How've you been?"

"Hanging in—barely. My drill sergeant hates my guts. She already owns my body; now she's after my soul. And there's six more weeks of it!"

"And the PT tests coming up."

"And the midcycle tests. And the gas chamber!" Paula cried. "I don't know . . ."

"You'll make it. You've got the guts."

She led the way back down the hall, back toward the church lounge. In a minute they'd be separated again. It was so damn frustrating, meeting like this, as if they were spies exchanging secrets.

They reentered the lounge. The men he'd come with were clustered against one wall, eyeing the women.

"Oh, oh . . ." Paula said, "Brunhilda's counting noses. I better go."

"How's the hand?"

"Fine."

"Take care." He touched her arm lightly as she turned away.

She smiled over her shoulder at him, surprised to see such kindness and hope in his face. "See you next Sunday?"

His face brightened into a warm grin. "You bet!"

Now why did I say that? she asked herself, confused by the pleasure she felt. And then she saw Thompson's inquisitive gaze shift from her to David, and she hurried back to her group.

14

CARVER FELT A SMALL SURGE of pride as he marched with his platoon, carrying the new guidon, white now, instead of red. The flags had been exchanged in a ceremony the week before, marking the end of the first two weeks of basic.

Somehow, they'd survived. O'Neill, ornery still, hadn't quit. Brown, though struggling, was holding his own. A couple of the guys who had trouble rope climbing and managing the overhead bars had come through, too, with his help.

As for him, he'd passed all the tests better than average. Except one—rifle fire. He could take the M-16 apart and put it back together, eyes closed. He could clean it better than the next guy. But firing it— scoring hits on the target—was another thing. He felt sick whenever he thought of the rifle proficiency test coming up.

What really hurt was that Monroe, who couldn't

zip up his own fly a couple of weeks ago, had turned out to be the best shot in the platoon. Figure that!

"Monroe!" the firing range instructor had shouted above the noise of the M-16 practice last Friday. "Over here!"

"I don't need help!" Carver had protested hotly.

"Listen, grunt! You *need* help! You couldn't hit a barn door from ten yards! Monroe! Over here on the double!"

Monroe had jogged to his side. The sergeant told him what to do, then went on down the line to check on the other trainees.

"Listen, Monroe! I don't *need* your help!" Carver had shouted over the noise of rifle fire. That smug white face reminded him of the parade of social workers who had tramped through his life, doling out money and food stamps with do-good smiles. He'd swung around and fired a few more rounds at the target to prove his point. None of them hit.

"Maybe your weapon isn't zeroed right," Monroe had said, reaching a hand out. "Let's have a look."

"Keep your cotton-pickin' hands away! I can zero my weapon as well as you!"

"What's the matter, Williams? You got a burr up your ass or something? How come you're all over the place helping this guy and that, but can't admit when *you* need help? Or is it just me you can't take it from?"

"Get lost! I don't need your fancy psychologizing!"

"Fine. Flunk the goddamn proficiency test for all I care. *Get* recycled. And while you're at it—*go to hell.*" Monroe had abruptly turned and gone back to his position on the firing range.

Be recycled? Carver thought as he cursed under his breath. Fear knotted his stomach. What if he didn't pass rifle marksmanship? He *couldn't, wouldn't* go through basic again! No! He'd pass, and without that Monroe's help, or anyone else's! He raised the M-16 to his shoulder once again, aimed carefully at the distant target, and fired.

"You need glasses?" the sergeant had shouted into his ear. "My two-year-old can do better'n that!"

Was it possible he *hadn't* zeroed the weapon properly, he thought now, shouldering his weapon on the exercise field. Could he swallow his pride and ask Monroe for help?

PAULA STEADIED HERSELF on the truck's bench seat as the vehicle taking them to their first experience with chemical warfare bounced over the rough road. The earth smelled of rot and mildew from the frequent rain, and the air felt heavy. Sticky with sweat, she tried to take her mind from her discomfort and fear by thinking of yesterday in church. Of David, and the way it had felt having his hand take hers.

"My *butt's* black and blue! Didn't the army never hear about cushions?" Tania asked.

"I don't know why *you* should complain, Tania," joked a very thin girl on a bench across the way. "You've got built-in cushions."

"Yeah. Least I got somethin' for a man to grab hold of," Tania shot back. "Not like you—flat butt!"

The girl leaped up and lunged at Tania.

"Way t' go!" Christine cheered.

"Hey . . . cut it out!" Paula threw herself between the two and grabbed the girl's arm. "Come on, sit down! We're all scared; that's all this is about. Let's not turn on each other."

Glaring, the girl retreated to her seat. In the awkward silence that followed, Tania's sweet, strong voice sang out unexpectedly—"*We shall overcome . . .*" Others joined in, and the tension eased.

Paula stared sadly at the passing landscape, wondering if men bickered and complained and scratched at each other the way women did. Last night, she'd been telling Christine about David and how she planned to skip Sunday services in the future so she wouldn't tempt the fates, when two of the girls got into a hair-pulling fracas over a tube of toothpaste! It was always something. And now this!

"Ah'm scared!" Christine whimpered as the truck pulled into the middle of a clearing before a tin shack. She shivered involuntarily. "What if I die?"

"You won't die. None of us will," Paula said, only half believing what she said.

"What if they leave us in the gas too long?"

"I, Tania Lester, do solemnly swear," Tania said, holding up two fingers, "that this is my last will and testament. I leave all of my worldly goods, including my full box of sanitary napkins, to— Man! The whole company's here!"

"Everybody out! Let's go!" a sergeant called, rapping the side of the truck with a stick. "Don't forget your gas masks! Fall in!"

Paula scrambled out of the truck and jogged with the rest of her platoon across the clearing to a large Quonset hut. The area was noisy with trucks arriving and soldiers disembarking. Would they put them all in one place and turn on the gas? What if your mask didn't work, or you were choking to death and they didn't notice?

The hand holding her gas mask shook. She hadn't felt fear like this at Thompson's wrath, or handling a grenade, or firing the M-16—but going into a room where poisonous gas would be pumped in, and you had no control over when they'd let you out, terrified her.

"What should you do if a nuclear bomb drops nearby?" one of the girls in the platoon asked. A hundred trainees were packed into the big Quonset hut while a specialist lectured on the effects of nuclear, biological, and chemical warfare.

"Put your head 'tween your knees, look up, and kiss the world good-bye!" Tania snickered.

"I heard that, grunt!" Sergeant Thompson called out. "That is *not* funny! If you expect to survive wartime, you better take this seriously!"

"Oh, man . . ." Tania whispered, rolling her eyes.

"The correct answer is—fall to the ground with your head away from the center of the blast and your rifle beneath you!"

Who has the sense of humor now? Paula wondered, picturing the scene.

"Any further questions?"

When no hands were raised, the instructor gave final instructions on how to put on the gas mask and what to expect if under chemical attack by an enemy. Then, platoon by platoon, they were led out of the building to a tin shack some distance away.

"This is it!" Christine said, face ashen. "Oh, God. If I die, who'll care for my baby?"

"Sergeant!" Tania called out. "My stomach hurts. I'm gonna be sick!"

The sergeant grinned. "Better not be, grunt, 'cause if you do you'll sure as hell make a mess in your gas mask!"

Logic said the army wouldn't deliberately poison a whole platoon of recruits, Paula thought. But that's not what her body said. Her stomach churned. Her mouth went dry. Her legs felt heavy and stiff, like logs. She shuddered.

Once more she checked to see if her mask was seated properly. Then, breathing hard, she commanded her body to move with the others into the building.

IT WAS A BARE ROOM, with high, dirty windows. David crowded in with the rest of his platoon. An exhilarating excitement raced through his veins. They looked like men from another planet with those clumsy masks over their faces. This was what being a soldier was all about! Not sit-ups and push-ups, cleaning latrines and making beds. This was the initiation ritual, the trial by fire. . . .

His heart pounded against his ribs. It felt so strange just standing there, waiting, wondering if the room was filling with gas yet, wondering if it had a smell and taste, if it would hurt your skin. Imagining what it could be like if you were on the battlefield, and the enemy used chemicals. Would you know in time to don your mask?

A whistle sounded, the signal to remove masks. He took a long, deep breath, yanked his off, and rattled off name, rank, and social security number amid a cacophony of other masculine voices. *Okay, open the doors now and let us out,* he thought. Tears sprang to his smarting eyes. His throat burned. A strange, unpleasant taste filled his mouth. Frantic, he took a breath and then another. Desperate, hands trembling, he tried to get the mask back on. Where was the exit? Why didn't they open the door like they were supposed to? He was dying!

"Everybody said his name, rank, and number?" a voice asked.

"Let us out!"

Someone unbolted a door to the outside. Through tearing eyes David saw daylight. Blindly, and gasping for breath, he stampeded with the others to the exit.

Outside at last, he gulped deep drafts of air, head thrown back, tears spilling down his cheeks. He couldn't breathe! He couldn't see! He tore at his itching skin, forgetting the warnings not to.

"Steady, Monroe. . . ." a voice said, giving him a supporting arm. "Steady. You'll be okay. Come on. . . ."

He leaned over and grasped his stomach, a wave of nausea coming so hard and fast, he started to heave and retch.

"Steady. . . . Take it easy. That's it. Just relax. Don't scratch!"

He leaned against the body and let himself be led away. "Sit here," the voice said. "That's it. Ease down. You'll be all right. Just don't scratch. Take this." He felt a canteen set in his hand, but tried to hand it back.

"Rinse your mouth. Wash your eyes. Here, I'll do it."

He felt cool water dabbed at his eyes. It eased the

terrible burning, but he still couldn't see clearly. He reached for the canteen and rinsed his mouth, spitting the water to the side.

"Better?"

He nodded, unable to speak.

"That was a damn fool thing to do—holding the mask over your face with all that gas still in the room!"

"What else could I do?" He coughed. "Breathe the goddamn stuff?" David opened his eyes and blinked to clear them. "*Williams?*"

"Yeah!"

He motioned to the coughing, retching soldiers nearby. "How come the gas didn't get *you*?"

"Black dudes can hold their breath longer than white dudes."

For a second he almost believed what he heard, then he grinned. "Yeah, sure. . . ."

"Feeling better?"

"A little."

"Good. Then get off your butt and let's go see if anyone else needs help."

the goodnight smile. David opened his eyes and blinked to clear them. "William . . .

CHAPTER

15

AS THEY RODE BACK to camp in the open trucks a light rain fell, cooling the air and cleaning away the last scent of gas.

"Man, that was *somethin'*. Thought they'd never let us out!"

"My eyes are still burning. . . ."

"I upchucked everything!"

"Me too."

"Imagine what it would be like if it was for *real*?"

Hearing the excited talk around him and feeling better, David's exhilaration returned. For the first time since coming to the camp he felt like a man, like a genuine *soldier*. It was an experience to write home about. He smiled to himself, glad he'd stuck it out.

He stole a glance at Williams, who sat opposite, observing but not contributing. Strange dude, he thought. Never complains. Works as hard or harder than anyone else. Stays to himself. Never talks about family (if he has one), or girls, like the rest of the guys.

Once, he'd heard Brown ask, "How come you never badmouth the sergeant, Williams?" And Williams had answered, "He's not so bad. Think about it. You can't have ten thousand *commanders* on the battlefield. All sarge's doing is teaching us to survive. We eat good, got clean beds, no rats or roaches; no drugs. . . . Could be worse."

David had glanced up in surprise. Good food, clean beds, no roaches or rodents were things you took for granted, weren't they? At least *he* did. Had he been *that* insulated and privileged, that *blind* to life in the black ghetto only a few miles away?

When the truck pulled into camp and they headed for the barracks, David made a particular effort to keep distance between him and Williams. He felt ashamed of having panicked. He'd been such a wimp, whining and throwing up like that!

Even worse, he owed Williams now. He didn't like being in debt to a guy who wouldn't let you pay back.

It was late afternoon. A platoon of red-faced, sweating grunts carrying full packs, led by a shouting, cursing drill sergeant, jogged around the track.

"One, two, three, four!" the drill sergeant sang out. "My buddy and me, we went to war!"

"Hey, Monroe. . . ." Williams called softly, suddenly at David's side. His dark skin glistened.

"Yeah, what?" David asked, maintaining his stride.

"I been thinking. I wouldn't mind if you gave me a few pointers on firing the M-16. Hate to pull the platoon's score down 'cause I can't shoot worth a damn. . . ."

David grabbed a surprised look in Williams's direction.

"If it's too much trouble, never mind!"

"No problem!" David returned quickly. "No problem! Next time we're on the firing range!"

"Swell." With that, Carver spurted ahead.

Well, what do you know, David thought to himself. The Iron Man is human after all.

THE SIGN over the open grave on the firing range said: VACANCY FOR—THE DAYDREAMER, UNBELIEVER, KNOW IT ALL, SLEEPER. DO YOU QUALIFY?

"*Do* you qualify?" the firing range instructor asked as they rode along in the open truck.

"No, *sir*!" David called out with the others.

"Lost a man just last month. Know how? Daydreamer, that's how. Rifle jams. So, what's he do? He turns around and shakes it real good then raises it to check it out and who's he got in his sites but the drill sergeant. And we all know you scumbags ain't got no great love for your drill sergeants." The instructor grinned knowingly at his audience, then crooked his right arm as if aiming and narrowed his eyes. "The sarge goes *kerpow*!" Get it? And that's how we lost the daydreamer. So listen up. You wanna stay alive, stay awake. . . ."

He's not gonna make it, David thought after a week of working with Williams. Williams knew it too.

"I don't know what's wrong!" he hissed. "I can't shoot worth a damn!"

"You're trying too hard, that's all. Relax!" It was odd. The guy was so good at all the physical stuff.

Learned the Smart Book faster than him. But unless he improved a hundred percent, he sure as hell would flunk marksmanship.

Williams clenched his teeth and raised his rifle again. Carefully, he took aim. "No good!" he exclaimed. "I get all shaky just before I pull the trigger."

"It's just a target, not a human being, fella!"

"That's just it. I keep seeing it as a guy like me or you!"

David didn't know what it took to be a good shot. Even as a kid his father had said he had a good eye and a steady aim. But with Williams, maybe it was something else. Something a guy couldn't have if he was training to be a killer. *Compassion.* That he might not have a killer instinct made him almost human, somehow.

Later the next week after Carver began showing some small improvement, they sat together in the barracks shining their boots. A quiet companionship had developed between them. David watched as his buddy slid an old nylon stocking over a boot. "Hey, where'd you learn to do that? It really makes a good shine; mind if I borrow it?"

Carver grinned slyly and passed the nylon to him. "Us darkies make the best shoeshine boys."

"Come off it, man. I don't see you as a shoeshine boy!"

"You don't know the first thing about me, Monroe."

"Because you won't let me!"

Carver nodded. He held his boot up to the light, spat lightly on one side and buffed it on his pant leg.

The smell of boot polish filled the room. "That's what Lavonne says. Says I don't let people close."

"Who's Lavonne?"

"My girl."

"I thought you had a lot of girls." David balanced his boot between his knees and tried to slide the nylon back and forth as Carver had.

"Not since Lavonne. Been going together two years now. How about you? What about your girl—what's her name? Bree?"

David lowered his right boot to the floor and picked up the left. The room was ablaze with light and busy with men straightening their lockers, studying, talking, writing letters. "Out of sight, out of mind, looks like. I've had one letter in three weeks."

"Sorry. Maybe she's sick or something!"

David shrugged. "Think she's got someone else already. Wasn't meant to be, I guess, but it sure hurts a guy's ego."

"If that's all it hurts, you're lucky." Carver stood up. "Be glad you didn't love her. Now, if I lost Lavonne. . . ." He didn't finish, but David got the message from the desolate look that crossed Carver's face. Then, as if embarrassed by revealing too much, he said, "See you later. Gotta shower before lights-out."

"Right."

David buffed his boot, thinking about what Carver had said. In the days he'd been helping him on the rifle range they'd gone from sparring partners to a tentative friendship, with a truce declared somewhere between. He'd been especially careful during the training sessions, not wanting to challenge Carver's pride. And in the end he'd come to admire the guy and even wish he could be more like him.

Still, it was hard to hide his irritation when Carver, despite everything he tried to teach him, kept scoring well below normal on the firing range. It didn't help, either, that the sarge kept threatening that anyone who didn't pass Rifle would be *recycled,* a punishment worse than a lifetime in hell—going through basic all over again.

RECYCLING. In civilian days Paula had turned in newspapers to be recycled to save trees. In army life the word had a completely new and menacing significance. It hung over her every day of basic. If she couldn't pass a test—cross a rope bridge in a specified time, treat someone in textbook order for gas inhalation or whatever, properly fire a rocket— she heard "Better shape up, Carlson, or you'll be recycled."

"Well, I'm not getting recycled and I'm not going to quit," she told Christine one day on bivouac. They were sitting under a tree downing their ready-to-eat lunch. "No matter how hard Thompson makes it for me I'm gonna get what I signed up for!" She swatted a mosquito, hearing the tone of desperation in her voice.

Christine placed a hand on her arm. "Sure you'll make it. Just don't let her get under your skin."

Paula wiped a tear from the corner of her eye with the back of a hand. She had thought Christine would crack, not her.

It was the third day in the field. Paula longed for a hot shower and clean bed. They had slept on the ground in sleeping bags in a damp grove of trees.

Marched in the rain carrying full packs and wearing ponchos that kept the wet out and the perspiration in. Crawled under barbed-wire fences on their bellies. Fired blanks over their buddies' heads as they tried to reach enemy bunkers into which they would lob grenades.

"Buddy ready?"

"Buddy ready."

"He's up! He's running. He's down. He's firing."

Forever after she would awake, cold with sweat, from dreams where she'd be running in slow motion, trying to zigzag through muddy fields, boots sticking in the mire, while fake bombs exploded nearby.

"Carlson! Get over here!"

She looked up to see the sergeant standing near the tent she shared with Tania.

"Look at that knot!"

Paula left her plate on a tree stump and hurried across the clearing. Setting up the tent had been left to Tania, her Ranger buddy. She should have checked the work; Tania was notoriously careless. Now it didn't matter who was responsible; as Ranger buddies they suffered equal blame and punishment.

"Is this your work?"

"Yes, ma'am," she said, furious for having to take the blame for something she hadn't done. She squatted to examine Tania's handiwork.

"What am I going to do with you, Carlson!" Thompson cried, loud enough for all to hear. "Can't even tie a simple knot! Too busy worrying about your hair, that's why!"

Paula felt the heat rise to her face. One more word about her hair and she'd wring that woman's neck!

Trembling with fury, she freed the last strand of rope and pulled the line taut. *Cool it!* she told herself. Take a deep breath and hold on! It she could just protect that kernel of self, of individuality, that Thompson seemed so intent on destroying, she'd survive.

"Carlson, you've got guard duty," the sergeant announced, with a sigh of exasperation. "Nine to midnight. Ranger buddy?"

"Yes, ma'am!" Tania responded, saluting smartly. "K.P. for the next two days!"

No longer hungry, Paula strode back to the tree stump for the rest of her rations. An army of ants had found its way to the beans and stew. She scraped the food into the trash and rinsed her plate.

Somehow she would get through these next weeks. She would not go back to civilian life without that educational bonus. That was a goal she had set and would meet. The harder Thompson pressed, the harder she would stand firm.

There was too much at stake—pride, self-image. Her very future.

CHAPTER

16

"A-TEN-SHUN!"

David, already standing at the foot of his bed awaiting inspection, drew to attention. In the six weeks he'd been here there had been numerous barracks checks, with the important ones on Saturday. Although adrenaline still flowed each time, the fear was nothing like it had been those first days and weeks. His buddies had united to monitor each other, determined to avoid the put-downs and penalties that came with careless barracks discipline.

"At ease!"

The big black sergeant stood at the entrance to the room with an uncharacteristic smile on his face. David stared. Something was wrong. Sarge looked positively human! For the first time he could imagine him married, maybe even somebody's father.

"All *right*! First—no inspection today." He

paused, a kind of smirk on his lips. "Thought that would get your attention!" Then he added, "Second —I want to commend you scumbags for scoring highest in Bravo Company on the rifle range this week."

David caught Carver's eye and smiled. The drill sergeants had allowed the poor shots in the platoon extra practice time. David had spent hours beside Carver, advising and encouraging. Yesterday they'd taken the qualifying test.

Carver had sat grim-faced and tight-lipped on the drive to the range. "Two more weeks to graduation. I may make it yet!" Telemantes said. "You got anyone coming to graduation, Williams?"

"What?" It was as if Carver were coming out of a trance. He shrugged.

David wished he could say something to ease Carver's anxiety, but there was no more to say or do. Now it was up to Carver. "You'll pass. Believe it!" David whispered just before they took positions. "Imagine Baker's face on that target and you'll do fine." He punched Carver lightly on the arm. "Good luck."

Afterward, David had rushed to Carver's side to learn his score. He didn't even have to ask. Carver's eyes had beamed amazement, relief and gratitude.

"For that reason," the drill sergeant went on, "I got a surprise—for y'all."

Sure, David thought. A twenty-five-mile hike, probably!

"You've done good. I don't say you're the best platoon in the company. But I'm not through with you, yet. Not by a long shot!

"Tonight, to show you I got a 'soft' side, and because I am proud of y'all, we're gonna have a little celebration. Just a little pizza party. Unless, of course, you'd rather eat in the mess hall?"

"No, Sergeant!" the cry went out.

The sarge grinned. "All right, men! You can order out from Pizza Perfect. Dis-missed!"

By evening, every time David thought about a big pizza with everything on it his mouth watered. He wanted a whole one all to himself. After weeks of mess hall chow, a pizza sounded better than Christmas dinner. O'Neill, who seemed to know the loopholes in every army regulation, offered to get beer from the officers' club. All in all, the evening couldn't fail.

"Pizza Perfect's got a policy," someone in the platoon announced when orders were taken. "If they can't deliver within forty-five minutes, you get it free. What do you think?"

"Yeah! That would be a charge!"

David could see the gears turning in everyone's head and immediately Telemantes said, "When we call in the order, we give 'em such complicated directions, they'll never make it in time."

"That's an old trick," one of the platoon squad leaders said. "Those guys must know all the tricks in the book."

"All *right*!" Carver suddenly exclaimed, eyes bright. "I got an idea! We order the pizzas—not for us, second platoon, Bravo Company—but for *Charlie* Company, down the road. . . ."

David understood Carver's plan instantly. "And we raid the pizza truck while the guy's inside delivering!" He laughed. "Great idea, Williams! You masterminded it—you take command!"

(129)

Gloria D. Miklowitz

"Somebody collect for the pizzas. Wouldn't want them to send the marines in after us."

"But what's the point?" Lee asked. "Why not get the pizzas delivered right here?"

"Too easy. No challenge. No fun."

"We'll draw straws for who goes," Carver said after no one else spoke up. "Shouldn't need more than six."

It was David's duty to call in the order. "Eight pizzas with everything on them; eight pepperoni; eight mushroom; four double cheese; four vegetarian —all large." He drew in an excited breath and tried to sound normal. "That's for Charlie Company, second platoon in C barracks. Know how to get there? Good. What's the tab? Fine. It'll be ready. Expect you by nine."

"Whoosh!" he said, hanging up. "They believed me!" He wiped sweat from his chin with one finger, forgetting he'd darkened his face with shoe black, and grinned.

"Okay, men," Carver said, looking over the camouflaged patrol. "Let's move it out."

Outside, darkness had fallen. The air smelled of damp earth and growing things. Carver tried to keep a straight face but a grin kept bubbling up. "Operation Pizza" they were calling this crazy raid. If the sarge found out, there'd be hell to pay. But what a kick, putting their skills to this use!

"We take the back route, stay off roads," he said when they assembled. "The idea is to go in without getting caught, scout the situation, capture the bunker, rescue the pizzas, and get back—while the pizzas are still hot. . . ." He chuckled.

They reached C barracks ten minutes before the

pizza van arrived. Carver motioned for half the patrol to move down-road from the brightly lit building, and half to remain with him.

David sat on his haunches, listening to the night
sounds and the mutter of voices from inside the barracks. It was weird, but he felt as high as if he were
really going into battle. "Bravo one to Bravo two," he
signaled over the radio, after a time. "Any sign of the
target yet?"

"Negative, Bravo one," the response came.
"Wait! Something's coming up the road now! Appears
to be. . . . it's them!"

"Bravo one to Bravo two. What is their troop
strength?"

"One, as far as I can tell—the driver. Should be in
range in a minute."

The pizza van pulled to a stop within fifteen feet
of Carver's patrol, just short of the entrance to C
barracks. Rock music blared from the van radio as
the driver, wearing an orange cap and jacket,
climbed out. Whistling and snapping his fingers, he
sashayed around to the side of the wagon and slid the
heavy door open. For a moment he stood looking at
the stacked boxes of pizza, scratching his arm. Then,
snapping his fingers, he went toward the building.

"He's gone in to get help carrying," David whispered.

"Who's got the money?" Carver asked.

One of the men raised a plastic bag full of coins
and dollar bills.

The door closed behind the delivery man. "Then
let's go!"

"Bravo one to Bravo two!" David excitedly signaled. "Operation Pizza under way. Come and get it!"

In a minute the six men converged on the van and emptied it of thirty-two boxes of hot pizzas.

"Wait. He's coming back! Let's see what happens!" Carver whispered, when they reached the security of the trees.

"I don't get it!" an irritated voice exclaimed. "I took the order myself. Charlie Company, C Barracks. That's what the guy said! I got it written down, right here!"

The delivery man and two soldiers left the building together and came to the van.

"I don't know. Maybe I read the address wrong. Maybe it's D barracks. You tell me." He led the soldiers to the side of the van. "What the devil!" He turned to the others. "They were here just a minute ago, I swear! Thirty-two boxes!"

"Let's go," Carver whispered, grinning in the darkness. "Before they follow their noses. . . ."

"Ta-dum!" Carver called out, leading the way into his own barracks ten minutes later. "Smell it and die!" He held high his load of pizza boxes.

"Oh, oh!"

Looming before them, arms crossed, was Drill Sergeant Baker. He looks like he could spit iron, David thought.

"Just where have you ladies been? Just what have you been up to?" the sergeant asked in a deceptively sweet voice.

"Er . . . uh . . . out getting the pizzas, Sarge!" Carver replied, unable to restrain a grin.

"Well, then. What are you standing there for, Private? No use letting good pizza get cold." He motioned to the six-packs on the floor beside him. "Or cold beer get warm. Let's have at it!"

The next morning when David's internal alarm woke him, it was still dark. Another minute and the sarge would come through clashing can lids or whatever. He closed his eyes, eager to catch every minute of sleep possible.

The next time he awoke the sky through the windows was bright. He leaped from bed, heart pounding, then realized everyone else was still asleep. Sarge must have gone soft, letting them sleep in on a Sunday.

The pizza party had gone on past midnight. Baker had let them smoke and drink beer, had joined in the jokes and storytelling. Had behaved like one of the guys. Afterward, David had told Carver, "I don't get it. How can I like the guy after the way he treated us these last six weeks?"

"Easy," Carver had said. "It's mind control. First you're belittled and terrorized till you're afraid to even breathe or you'll be punished without knowing what for. Then, since you don't like pain, you learn pretty quick what your captor expects. Eventually, you'll do anything just for a little pat on the head, a little pizza party."

"Yeah," David had said. "I see what you mean."

Now he rose from bed and made his way to the latrine. Church services at ten. The highlight of the week. He always went hoping, hoping Paula would come, but she hadn't yet, not since that first time.

Maybe today!

"WHERE WILL YOU GO when you finish basic?" he asked. He'd seen Paula slip out of her seat during the service and a moment later, followed. They stood, now, in the hallway near the phones. He felt the same electric excitement between them that he'd sensed that day on the plane.

"Wherever they give specialized training in journalism. But the way things are going, I may not graduate. I have nightmares that Thompson, my drill sergeant—we call her Brunhilda—will stand over me during finals and laugh."

He nodded. "Baker's the same way—or was until last night. Say, why haven't you been in church these last weeks?"

Paula looked away. "I don't like sneaking around and whispering like this. If we're caught, it's K.P. or worse."

She hadn't answered his question, but he let it go. "I feel like we'd have a thousand things to say to each other, if we had time. Don't you?"

"Listen, David. I have no room in my life for a man right now! Maybe not for a long while—until I'm through with the army."

"I'm not asking you to marry me, Paula," David said, smiling.

Paula blushed.

"Can't we be friends? Write to each other? Call each other from time to time? Maybe see each other when we get leave?"

"I don't know. I really can't plan anything until I get through basic. Then, I'll see. . . ."

"You'll pass. I bet you're the kind who always thinks she's flunking, then gets all A's." He touched her arm. "Let's make a date—have a drink together after graduation."

"Maybe. Yes," she said, returning his smile. "That

would be nice. Now, I think we better go back before we're missed."

He let her go first so it wouldn't be obvious they'd been together. She was tall and trim, with a kind of bounce to her step. And her hair was so beautiful, fine, like a baby's, and alive, with all the colors of fire. He imagined removing her cap and slowly, slowly undoing the pins that held those thick, rich ropes of flame.

He watched her disappear into the chapel and started down the hall. How unsatisfying to meet like this! He wanted time, a place to be together, music playing, good food between them. They would talk. About home, hers and his. About his father, who had written only once in the nearly seven weeks, calling him stupid for joining up when he could have gone to college on Charlie's money.

He'd like to tell her about his stepfather, and how he'd detested him enough to join the army. And yet, now, all those feelings seemed so vindictive, so adolescent.

He'd like to ask if these weeks in the army had made her think or feel different from before. Because, he realized with surprise, he did—felt a lot different, in ways he hadn't yet quite defined.

17

"ARE YOU READY to take the challenge?" a disembodied voice called in the darkness.

"Yes!" David screamed, his voice one of hundreds.

"Can't hear you!"

"*Yes!*" the voices rang out again.

"Are you *sure*?"

"*Yes, yes!*"

David could barely make out Brown's short body in front of him, and beyond and behind, others—the whole Bravo Company. They had crawled on their bellies over rocks and gravel to get oriented for this night infiltration course. Now they stood in a ten-foot-deep trench in total darkness, awaiting the signal to go.

"Are you *certain*?" the same voice shouted.

"*Yee*ess. . . ." The answer petered out to a frightened whisper as a blast of flares and TNT explosions began. Rockets whooshed flatly across the horizon, zinging over the dimly lit barbed wire. Machine guns, spitting red tracer rounds and thousands of bullets, swept the plain they would have to cross.

David gripped his rifle, eyes straining, mouth dry, steadily moving down the trench to another where men lined up behind log ladders. They were expected to climb up the ladders, roll over a horizontal log, and crawl the treacherous course on their bellies with rifles and full packs. They had been told that the machine guns were bolted in place and fired only down alleys where no one would crawl, but to David it didn't seem possible. In the light of a flare, he peered out of the trench before launching himself over the top. He saw bullets strike sandbags and heard an apocalyptic roar that sent a shudder of terror down his spine.

Brown, just ahead of him, hesitated, half his body raised lizardlike above the trench. "Shit! This is suicide!"

"Lane twenty-three! Get going!" the sergeant barked.

David pushed Brown forward, then squirted over the top himself and lay panting, hugging the flat ground.

He saw the course clearly now, lit again by a flare. It was strewn with barbed wire, bunkers, shallow trenches, booby traps, and smoke bombs. Rockets whizzed by, and machine-gun bullets ripped the air. And slithering steadily through it all were hundreds of soldiers, like an army of slow-moving turtles.

"Shit," Brown exclaimed as a new flare lit the course. He buried his face in the dirt.

David's teeth chattered. The flare's light

dimmed. "Move!" he said, conscious of the men pouring out of the trenches behind him.

Brown whimpered and curled into a fetal position.

David elbowed forward. "Brown, get going! Before the next flare! Move!"

"Can't! Go without me!"

"Move, damn you! I'll stay beside you. Now, move!" He jabbed the muzzle of his rifle into Brown's arm.

Brown rose slightly and inched forward as another flare lit the sky. And with it, the deafening roar of a half-pound block of TNT detonating in a nearby bunker. He dropped flat, and shivering, began to sob.

David bit his tongue. *Help! Ma—help!* he cried silently. Sweat poured down his arms. He squeezed his eyes shut and prayed, *God, please don't let me die!* And then, as the flare fizzled, he grabbed Brown's shoulder straps and dragged him, eating dust, cringing at the whine of the rockets overhead, but moving, moving forward. Until—panting, arms aching—he reached a barbed-wire fence and Brown suddenly yanked free.

"It's okay now! Let go! I'm all right now," he said. He drew even with David, reached back into his pack for the wire clippers, and set to work.

Later, David marveled at it all. Why had he risked his own skin to help Brown? Where had he found the strength? How come, despite the terror, he'd pushed on anyway? When had the lessons of these last weeks become so much a part of him that when faced with danger he'd react immediately and appropriately?

* * *

THE NIGHT BEFORE end-of-cycle tests Paula lay wide awake, unable to sleep. Everything she'd learned ran through her head again and again. Tomorrow—maybe it was already tomorrow—her fate would be decided. It was unreasonable to believe she'd fail—but there were so many ways to foul up. A lot of it was so technical and you could fail only two tests of twenty. Plus, Thompson had made it perfectly clear that passing basic meant more than passing tests, too. It meant walking like a man, talking like a man, looking like a man. Total subservience to her and the system.

Maybe she *should* have cut her hair; hair grew back. Maybe she'd flaunted her femininity somehow. If she had it to do over again, she wouldn't be so stubborn.

Not true.

She sighed and curled into a position that usually induced sleep. She *had* to be in top form in a few hours. Just thinking that brought on a surge of adrenaline. *Sleep!*

Think about Dan and the good times together. That might help. Right! She called up Dan's handsome face, but the first memory to surface was the one that hurt most. The time they were sharing a two-bedroom apartment with two "Valley Girl" types, Dan's characterization. She'd returned to their apartment for a book she'd forgotten one day, and found him in *their* bed with one of them.

David Monroe. Her inflamed mind discarded Dan and tried out the new name for comfort. She hardly knew him and he was probably a year younger than she—yet . . . there was a chemistry.

She flipped onto her back, crossed her arms and

stared up at the ceiling. *Why was she thinking about men, anyway?* She'd sworn off them. You didn't need a man to be happy! *She* didn't!

But. If she passed finals, David Monroe had said they'd have a drink together at graduation to celebrate. They could get to know each other slowly, through letters and phone calls and visits instead of jumping into a relationship just because of hormones.

She smiled at the ceiling and turned to her side. What would it be like kissing him? she wondered.

ALL THAT WORRY, Paula huffed, running the last lap of the PT finals. And it was nothing! All her life she'd been a compulsive overpreparer, a worrier. David had been right. She *was* the kind who always thought she'd fail, then to her great surprise, wound up with A's.

She reached the end of the course, face burning and dripping sweat, but to her amazement felt she still had more to give. "Good time," Thompson allowed, consulting a stopwatch and writing it down while Paula jogged to a tree, leaned against it, and unscrewed the top of her canteen.

She'd passed everything. She'd added the scores in her head, but it wasn't until late that afternoon she learned for sure. Thompson had marched them around the dusty field for what seemed hours. "Met him on a Sunday and my heart stood still," they sang with the drill sergeant alternating the verses as she strode beside the platoon. "The do-run-run, the do-run-run. Someone told me he was the senior drill. The do-run-run. . . ."

"Privates Carlson, Fahey, and Hyland," Thompson called, bringing the platoon to a halt. "Step forward."

Paula strode to the front of the platoon, heart fluttering. What did Thompson want with her now? She came to a halt directly in front of the drill sergeant, and stood at attention, squinting into the afternoon sun.

"At ease!"

Paula shifted position, eyeing the sergeant warily.

"First, I'd like to say I'm proud of you all. Seven weeks ago you were slovenly, undisciplined, hopelessly ineffective, whining babies. Today all of you passed the final tests that complete your basic training. I am proud of you. Very proud!" She beamed.

Paula had a sudden insight. Except for those who quit, or the two girls who had been given discharges because they were hopeless misfits, no one would be recycled. The army didn't want anyone to fail. That's why you could retest almost endlessly. If she'd only known that in the beginning! How much worry it would have saved.

"I'd like to especially commend these three soldiers," Thompson said, bringing Paula's attention back. "Privates Carlson, Fahey, and Hyland scored highest in the platoon in overall performance. I'd match them skill for skill against any man in the U.S. Army!" She thrust a hand out to Paula. "Congratulations, Private Carlson! Thought I'd never see the day." She pumped Paula's hand with manly vigor.

"Thank you, Sergeant Thompson."

"When ya gonna get that hair cut?"

Paula laughed. "When I'm good and ready."

Thompson shook her head, but smiled. Then she

offered her hand to the next soldier. "Congratulations, Private Fahey."

I did it, Paula thought, wanting to scream out to everyone how great she felt.

"Dis-missed!" Thompson called.

Paula swung around and marched back to formation, grinning. Christine winked at her. Tania gave her a thumbs-up. She must look awful after all she'd gone through today—uniform filthy, face streaked with dirt, hair a mess, boots caked with mud.

But—oh, she sure felt *wonderful*!

CHAPTER

18

"MAN, AIN'T I *somethin'*!" Carver exclaimed. "Lavonne gonna flip!" He grinned at his image in the mirror. He was wearing dress greens and his shirt was immaculate; the crease in his trousers, razor sharp; his low quarters reflected the light every way he turned.

David beamed too. Graduation day. He stuck out his chest, saluted his image, readjusted the cap, and laughed when his eyes met Carver's in the mirror. "Unh-unh!" he said, imitating Carver's black jive. "Ain't *we* somethin'!"

"You grunts, stop kissin' the mirror! Get yo' ugly faces outta the way!" O'Neill cried, edging around David's head. "Let a handsome dude like me have a look!"

For most of the week before, they had gone through endless marches and drills, routines that had become automatic. All in preparation for graduation. Baker had even eased up, ignored conduct he would have dropped them for the first weeks.

David had begun counting the days, the hours to graduation. His family were *all* coming, Heather, Mom, and Charlie. And *Dad*—from New York! And best of all he'd have time to be with Paula without having to constantly check over his shoulder.

"Ten-shun!"

David scurried to the front of his bunk and stood at attention. It was the last inspection before graduation.

"At ease, men!"

Sergeant Baker strode into the room, briskly checked each of their uniforms, stared hard at O'Neill, eyes narrowed, then moved on. David suppressed a grin, remembering the chaos of his first inspection.

"Lookin' good, men," the drill sergeant said. "You'll all be moving on to specialized training by tomorrow, so I may not get another chance to say— good luck! You'll make mighty fine soldiers. I'm proud of you!" He cleared his throat. "Now, form up outside and let's get this thing over with!"

Two companies were graduating—Bravo and Charlie; eight platoons in all, nearly three hundred and twenty men. As David marched with his platoon to the parade ground he felt so full of joy and excitement, he thought he might laugh aloud.

"Standin' tall, lookin' good!" Baker sang out.

"Standin' tall, lookin' good!" David echoed.

"Oughta be in Hollywood!"

"Yeah!"

David nudged Carver as they formed up on the

field and stood at ease. "You see Lavonne?" Impossible, of course; the people in the distant stands were a blur of color.

"Sure do! See those yellow balloons way up high? That'll be her!"

David swallowed a lump in his throat. Somewhere in those stands sat Heather, with his mom and Charlie. His father had promised to fly in from New York. And then yesterday, as he should have expected, canceled. "Sorry," the telegram read, "urgent new assignment prevents trip. Congratulations, you chip off the old block." At first he'd felt some of the same anguish that came whenever his father promised and didn't deliver. He'd even started justifying his father's excuse. But then he'd stopped. *Chip off the old block*, huh? No. He didn't think so.

"Atten-tion!"

David stood tall.

"Post colors!"

Four flagbearers proceeded to the front of Bravo and Charlie companies and about-faced. On either side of them stood a soldier bearing a rifle.

"All stand for the pledge of allegiance!"

There was a stir in the stands as the hundreds of visitors rose to their feet. David placed his hand over his heart. How often he'd given the pledge mechanically, not letting the meaning penetrate. But now, as the words echoed through loudspeakers on the field, he shivered. And when the army band played "The Star-Spangled Banner," his eyes filled with tears.

He squinted in the bright sun, as plaques and trophies were awarded and one after another top brass were introduced. Speaking from a podium on the field, they told of the army's important role in defending freedom, and of the pride the families and friends of these "fine young men" should feel. As the speeches droned on, David's mind wandered.

Strange, he thought, how close I feel to the men in my squad, closer than to any friends I made in high school. With basic over, they'd all scatter. First they'd be sent for specialized training. Carver would be off to a course in aircraft mechanics. He and O'Neill would be leaving tonight for Ranger training. Brown would school as a computer systems analyst. Lee was going into Intelligence. Afterward, they'd be assigned wherever the army needed them for the rest of their enlistment. He stole a sideways glance at Carver. I'm gonna miss that dude most of all, he thought with a pang of regret.

"Pass in review! Column right, *march*!"

David stepped along at the prescribed pace, eyes on the head in front.

"Column left, *march*!"

When he reached the stands, Baker called, "Eye —*right*!"

Marching briskly, with head turned toward the bleachers, David scanned the faces. So many people straining to identify their soldier sons, husbands, or friends. Where was Mom? Heather? Was that Charlie? Could they recognize him, or did all the soldiers look alike with their clean-shaven faces, same haircuts, same uniforms? Where was Paula? Had she already passed in review, or was she behind him? His pulse jumped as he thought of the appointment they'd made to meet later.

CARVER PUSHED THROUGH the crowd of soldiers and visitors looking for Lavonne. With so many men and their families, it was a wonder anyone found his own. He searched now for the yellow balloons high above the crowd. Lavonne had come up with the idea. Where they were, there she'd be. He passed Telemantes embracing a girl who looked like the photo he always carried. And then he spotted the bouquet of yellow off to one side. His heart thumped loudly in his throat.

"Carver! Wait! Meet my family!" David called, grabbing his arm in passing. "Mom. Heather. Charlie. Meet Carver Williams. My buddy. He's from Pasadena!"

"Happy to meet you, Carver," Mrs. Monroe said, holding out a hand. "*Davey* has written so much about you."

"*David*, Mom . . ."

"Pleased to meet you, ma'am," Carver said, but his eyes slid over their heads to the balloons.

"Yeah, yeah. *Lavonne.* I know. Go on," David said, giving him a push. "See you later."

Lavonne! Carver struggled through the crowd, eyes always on the balloons. And then, breaking through a cluster of people, suddenly, there she was, her satin-smooth skin wrapped in a pale yellow sundress. His throat tightened.

"Lavonne!" He leaped forward and grabbed her up in his arms. "Lavonne!"

"Carver!" The balloons floated free, and she was laughing and crying, and hugging and kissing him the way he had pictured a hundred times in the last weeks.

"Hey, soldier, how about a hug for your sister?" He opened his eyes to see Kisha, hair done in cornrows, dancing up and down.

Gloria D. Miklowitz

"Kisha, honeybun!" Grinning, so filled with happiness he thought he might burst, he lowered Lavonne to the ground and encircled her waist with an arm. "Come give yo' big brother a hug!" He grabbed his sister around the waist with his other arm. "Got the two prettiest girls in Alabama—all to myself!"

"You look good, Carver. Real good," his mother exclaimed, tears in her eyes. "Don't he, Deon?"

"Sure does . . ."

He glanced at Kisha, trying to gauge what might be going on between her and Deon, but couldn't tell. "Hey, let's get outta this circus and go someplace to talk."

"Deon rented a car," his mother said proudly. "When you gotta be back?"

"Seven, tomorrow." Carver leaned his cheek against Lavonne's. Her skin felt warm, and she smelled sweet, like a peach freshly picked. "We got the whole night!" he whispered into her ear. The look she returned was so full of love that his legs felt weak. He could hardly wait for them to be alone.

"BREE COULDN'T COME. Charlie invited her, offered to pay the fare . . ." David's mother explained, fanning herself with the paper program from graduation. They were threading their way through the mass of visitors toward the parking lot.

"She was very busy with midterms; you remember how it was," Charlie offered.

"That's okay," David said, turning to look back. "I know she's seeing someone else. It doesn't matter." He caught a quick look of relief pass between his mother and Charlie. "Hey, there's my drill sergeant.

(148)

You gotta meet him! What a guy! Remember what I wrote? Well, I know him better now. Soft as butter under that tough shell!

"Sergeant Baker!" he called, but the sergeant disappeared into the crowd.

"We've got champagne in our hotel room," his mother said, "and all sorts of goodies. Bet you haven't had a decent meal since you left home!"

David put a loving hand on his mother's arm. "Do I look like they starved me?"

When they reached the parking lot, he said, "I have to see a friend. Mind if I join you later? You'd probably like a little rest anyway, after sitting in that hot sun all morning." He checked his watch. Paula would be waiting. Soon she'd be leaving too. He had to get her address so they could keep in touch and see each other again. "Where are you staying?"

"Bring your friend along," Charlie said, naming their hotel.

"Maybe I will." David held out his hand. "And thanks, Charlie. Thanks for everything."

"For what?" Charlie asked, his face reddening. "No thanks necessary, m'man!" He stuck out his hand.

His mother smiled, then reached up and pecked David on the cheek. She climbed into the rental car and looked out. "Now, don't be too long, soldier boy."

"*Man*," Charlie corrected.

David slammed the car door and watched until Charlie drove off. And then he turned back toward the camp.

Paula!

He quickened his step until he was running.